Airy Fairy's

Book of Magic

Margaret Ryan
illustrated by Teresa Murfin

SCHOLASTIC

Scholastic Children's Books,
Euston House, 24 Eversholt Street,
London NW1 1DB, UK
a division of Scholastic Ltd
London ~ New York ~ Toronto ~ Sydney ~ Auckland
Mexico City ~ New Delhi ~ Hong Kong

First published in the UK in this edition by Scholastic Ltd, 2005

Magic Mischief!

To Sophie Jean Elizabeth
Love from Margaret Ryan

Chapter One

It was school report day at Fairy Gropplethorpe's Academy for Good Fairies, and Airy Fairy's least favourite day of the year.

"My report's sure to be awful," she muttered to her friends, Buttercup and Tingle. "I wish we didn't get them just before the holidays."

"Perhaps it won't be as bad as you think," whispered Buttercup.

"Try not to worry about it," murmured Tingle.

"Do sit up straight and stop talking, Airy Fairy," frowned her teacher, Miss Stickler. "I never met such a girl for sprawling and muttering."

"Sorry, Miss Stickler," said Airy Fairy, and sat up straight and folded her arms.

"Now, pay attention, Fairies," said Miss Stickler, "while I read out your reports. Some of them are very very good." And she beamed at Scary Fairy, who was her niece, and always top of the class. "And some of them are very very bad." And she glared at Airy Fairy, who was always at the bottom.

Airy Fairy gave a huge sigh. It was always the same. Scary Fairy got everything right while she got everything wrong. It wasn't that she didn't try. It was just that things didn't work out somehow. Take last week, for instance. All the fairies were in the school hall preparing for the end of term concert. Everyone had a special job to do. Buttercup had magicked up the chairs, Tingle had magicked up the programmes, and Airy Fairy had been asked to magic up ten red coats for the school choir. But the spell went wrong when she sneezed in the middle, and she magicked up ten red goats instead. Ten badly behaved red goats.

They charged all round the hall, knocked over the chairs and ate the programmes. When Fairy Gropplethorpe arrived to magic them away, they biffed her on the behind and ate her wand. Then they knocked over Miss Stickler who was carrying a large vase full of flowers.

The vase and Miss Stickler crashed to the ground, and the goats galloped past them into the dining room, and polished off the school dinners. Then they trotted into the classroom and ate all the fairies' spelling books too. Airy Fairy didn't mind that. Her spelling was as dodgy as her magic.

But Fairy Gropplethorpe wasn't pleased, and Miss Stickler was furious about her best vase. Airy Fairy sighed just thinking about it. She didn't mean to cause trouble. It just seemed to follow her around.

She sighed again and looked out of the classroom window. A wintry sun shone on Fairy Gropplethorpe's Academy for Good Fairies and turned it to gold. To human beings the school just looked like an abandoned tree house, perched high up in an old oak, but it was home to ten tiny fairies.

"You are here to learn to do good fairy magic, Fairy Gropplethorpe had told them on their first day at school, "so that when you leave to go out into the world you can make it a better place. The humans have rather messed it up," she added sadly.

"You will also uphold the reputation of the school," said Miss Stickler, "as the very best in the country for good fairy magic. Is that clear?"

"Yes, Miss Stickler," all the fairies had chanted.

But some of them learned more quickly than others.

"Airy Fairy, will you stop looking out of the window and pay attention!"

"What? I mean, pardon? I mean, what did you say, Miss Stickler?"

"I said you haven't been listening to a word I've been saying. No wonder you're at the bottom of the class."

Scary Fairy, who sat behind Airy Fairy, giggled, and gave her a sly poke with her wand.

"Stupid. Stupid," she chanted.

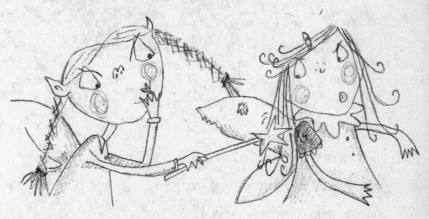

Miss Stickler picked up Airy Fairy's school report between finger and thumb and held it away from her.

"Just look at this report, Airy Fairy," she said. "Nothing out of ten for spelling."

"It doesn't make any sense to me," said
Airy Fairy. "Why does pond have an 'o' in
the middle while wand has an 'a'?"

"Nothing out of ten for magicking."

"The goats were a little mistake," said Airy
Fairy. "It was an accident."

"Nothing out of ten for flying," went on
Miss Stickler.

"I didn't see the window," said Airy Fairy.
"I think all windows should have coloured
glass in them, to let you know they're there.
Or maybe have flowers painted on them.
Pansies, I think. That would be nice. Or

"Airy Fairy!" yelled Miss Stickler. "We are
not talking about eyesight. We are talking
about your school report."

"Yes, Miss Stickler. Sorry, Miss Stickler."

"A school report that is so awful Fairy
Gropplethorpe wants to see you in her study
right away."

"Oh no," gasped Buttercup and Tingle.

"Yes, Miss Stickler," sighed Airy Fairy, and
trailed out to the front of the class.

On her way, she knocked over the table with the brushes and the paint pots.

"Oops, sorry," said Airy Fairy, and stopped to pick them up.

Scary Fairy pretended to help her.

"What an idiot you are," she whispered. "I bet Fairy Gropplethorpe gives you a terrible row. I bet she breaks your wand in two. She might even expel you!" And she gave Airy Fairy a sly nip.

Airy Fairy yelled and dropped a paint pot on Scary Fairy's toe.

"Do be careful, Airy Fairy," said Miss Stickler. "Scary Fairy's trying to help you. And pull up your socks and straighten your wings, and try to look like a fairy should. Dainty and pretty and TIDY."

"Yes, Miss Stickler," said Airy Fairy, and opened the classroom door.

"And don't bang the door."

"No, Miss Stickler," said Airy Fairy. But a gust of wind whistled along the corridor at that moment, and the classroom door banged shut and the handle fell off.

"Airy Fairy!" yelled Miss Stickler.

But Airy Fairy was too busy worrying about what Fairy Gropplethorpe would say to hear.

Airy Fairy made her way down the long corridor and the creaky flight of stairs to Fairy Gropplethorpe's study, and knocked on the door.

"Enter," boomed a voice.

Airy Fairy took a deep breath and went inside.

Fairy Gropplethorpe was sitting at a large desk in front of an open fire. An old dog lay warming himself on the hearth. Fairy Gropplethorpe had found him in a Christmas cracker years ago and had magicked him alive. He thumped his tail when he saw Airy Fairy.

"Hullo, Macduff," said Airy Fairy.
Macduff heaved himself on to his paws,
knocked over the fire irons with his tail, and
came to greet Airy Fairy. He licked her hands
as she tickled behind his slightly singed ears.

Fairy Gropplethorpe shook her head.

"This is not a social call, Airy Fairy," she said. "I am concerned about your school report. It is not good."

"No, Fairy Gropplethorpe," sighed Airy Fairy, and stared at her pink fairy shoes. One of them had come undone so she bent down to fix it.

"Airy Fairy? Where are you? Where did you go? What ARE you doing?" said Fairy Gropplethorpe.

"Sorry," said Airy Fairy, and stood up quickly and bumped her head on Fairy Gropplethorpe's desk.

"Do try to pay attention, Airy Fairy," sighed Fairy Gropplethorpe. "And just look at the state of you. Your frock is grubby. Your knees are scraped. Your wings are bent and covered in sticking plaster. I suppose that happened in flying class."

Airy Fairy nodded and scuffed her toes on the carpet.

"A fairy must learn to LOOK where she's flying," said Fairy Gropplethorpe. "Not at everything else round about. She must learn to GLIDE through doorways. Not dive-bomb them. How you will cope with revolving doors when we do them next term I shudder to think."

Airy Fairy hung her head.

"Your magic class was a disaster too," Fairy Gropplethorpe added. "You got your spells wrong, didn't you?"

Airy Fairy nodded. "Sometimes I say a word wrong. Sometimes I spell a word wrong. And sometimes I just forget what I started out to do..."

Fairy Gropplethorpe shook her head.

"And I suppose you've bent your wand again."

Airy Fairy nodded once more.

"Let me see."

Airy Fairy held it out.

Fairy Gropplethorpe tutted.

"Wands should be straight, Airy Fairy,"
she said, taking it from her and fixing it.
"They should not be able to point round
corners. You've been poking people with it,
haven't you?"

Airy Fairy nodded again. Scary Fairy
always picked on her, and had poked her
first, but as usual, Airy Fairy had been the
one Miss Stickler had caught.

"Well," said Fairy Gropplethorpe. "I know it's almost the holidays, but this report is so bad that I'm afraid you leave me no choice. You will have to do some extra work before you can attend the school party on Christmas night. While all the other fairies are busy getting the hall ready you will go and spend some time as a tree fairy."

"Oh no," cried Airy Fairy. "Not a tree fairy. Not spend time on top of a prickly tree with pine needles sticking in my bottom! That's awful. I promise I'll do better in school, Fairy Gropplethorpe. I promise I'll try harder."

22

"Too late, Airy Fairy. I'm sorry, but you must learn to pay more attention in class. Now here is the address of the family you have to go to.

"Their name is Grimm, and they are grim in more ways than one. Most human beings try to be nicer to each other at this time of year, but not the Grimms. They will be a real test of your good fairy magic. If you have managed to learn any! You have six chances to try to improve the Grimms. Six spells to make them into nicer people before Christmas night. You will stand at the top of their Christmas tree and do your very best.

"I shall be keeping an eye on you, and, if you succeed, you can go to the party. If not, then I'm afraid you'll be in bed early. Do you understand?"

"Yes, Fairy Gropplethorpe," sighed Airy Fairy.

"Just try really hard, Airy Fairy," Fairy Gropplethorpe smiled. "I'm sure you can do it."

Airy Fairy trailed back to her class to tell Miss Stickler what Fairy Gropplethorpe had said.

"Well, perhaps this will teach you a lesson, Airy Fairy," said Miss Stickler. "Twenty-three Fairly Close isn't far away, but you'd better set off now, before it gets dark."

Airy Fairy turned to go.

"You can do the good fairy magic, Airy Fairy," said Tingle. "I know you can."

"Just remember the spells," said Buttercup. "You'll get to the party."

"I bet you won't," sneered Scary Fairy. Then she muttered to herself, "I'll make very sure of that."

Chapter Two

Airy Fairy set off for the Grimms', feeling miserable. "What a way to spend Christmas," she sighed. "It's bad enough being an orphaned fairy without being stuck up on top of a tree as well. Now where did I put that piece of paper with the address on it?"

She was so busy searching in her pockets and up her sleeves that she didn't see the big puddle by the side of the road.

And she certainly didn't see the big bus coming along.

WHOOSH! The bus went through the puddle. SPLOOSH! The water sprayed all over Airy Fairy.

"Oh no," she cried. "I'm soaked."

Water dripped from her hair, water dripped from her dress, water dripped from her nose.

She stood there shivering till a friendly cat gave her a ride on his back to twenty-three Fairly Close.

Airy Fairy blew a thank you into his ear and slid to the ground. She made her way to the front door, and let herself in through the bad-tempered letter box, which snapped shut on her fingers, and tore her pink fairy frock.

"Oh crumbs," said Airy Fairy. "Now everyone can see my pink knickers. I'll have to fix my frock." And she meant to do the spell for fixing frocks, but somehow it came out as the spell for stitching socks, and, when she looked, she had ten tiny socks stitched on the side of her fairy frock.

"Oh crumbs," said Airy Fairy again, and managed to do the spell to remove them. Then she looked around her at twenty-three Fairly Close. There was nobody home except for a cat and dog snoozing on the sofa, and a hamster who came out of his bed, filled his cheeks with peanuts, then went back to sleep.

"Right," said Airy Fairy. "I suppose I'd better get myself up on top of that Christmas tree."

The huge Christmas tree was standing at a drunken angle by the sitting room window. Its lower branches were covered in gold tinsel, its middle branches were covered in blue tinsel and its upper branches were covered in red tinsel. Only the spiky topmost branch was bare.

"Just waiting for me, I suppose," sighed Airy Fairy. "I wonder if my wings are working properly yet."

She took off from the orange and purple carpet, flew in a circle and … missed the tree completely. DOINNNNG! She hit the window and slid down on to the ledge.

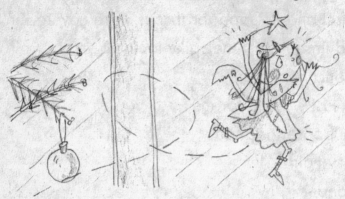

"Wings are still wonky then," she muttered. "Perhaps I should try taking off from the arm of that green chair. That should give me a bit of a lift."

She huffed and puffed up on to the arm of the chair and took off. Downwards.

She hit a football which carried her across
the room and deposited her in the fireplace.

Soot fell down the chimney on to her head.
Airy Fairy wiped her face with her frock.

"Could do better, Airy Fairy," she
mimicked Miss Stickler's voice. "Perhaps
if I climb up the curtain."

She huffed and puffed up
the curtain, grabbed the
curtain cord, and
swung across
like Tarzan.

Oouu-oouu-oo-ouch! She landed in the middle of the Christmas tree, in among the thickest, prickliest branches. She hit a shiny yellow bauble, slid down a spiky tinsel star and came to a halt on top of a wobbly red Santa who started to sing "We wish you a Merry Christmas," and gave her the fright of her life.

"I've a terrible feeling," she said, as she started the long climb up to the top of the tree, "that this isn't going to be a very merry Christmas at all."

Chapter Three

Airy Fairy had just got to the top of the tree when the family arrived home. She remembered to stand up straight and smile vacantly just in time.

Darren Grimm eyed her narrowly.

"I don't remember that tree fairy being there before we went out," he said.

"Course it was," said his twin sister, Dawn. "Don't you know anything? All Christmas trees have a fairy on the top."

"No, they don't," yelled Darren.

"Yes, they do," yelled Dawn.

"Be quiet, you two," said their mum, struggling in with the Christmas cake in one hand and a large turkey in the other.

"Give it a rest," said their grandma."It's nearly Christmas."

"Can we open the presents under the tree then?" said Darren.

"No," said his mum.

"Not till tomorrow," said Dawn. "It's not Christmas till tomorrow. Don't you know anything."

"I know more than you, Clever-clogs."

"Stop it right now," yelled their mum. "Or Christmas will be cancelled. Darren, take the dog out for a walk. He's hopping about cross-legged."

"Not my turn," smirked Darren. "It's hers."

"It's not. It's his."

"It's not. I took him this morning."

"That was yesterday. I took him this morning."

"Liar liar, pants on fire!"

Airy Fairy watched in amazement as the twins pushed and poked at each other. Then she heard the dog give a deep sigh and lift his leg on the Christmas tree.

"I don't believe it," she muttered. "I know Fairy Gropplethorpe said the Grimms were grim, but this is awful."

"Now look what you've made the dog do," Mum yelled at the twins. "Get a mop and clean up that mess, Darren."

"It was her fault," said Darren.

"No, it wasn't. It was his fault," said Dawn.

"Oh dear," muttered Airy Fairy. "I think I'll have to use one of my six spells to fix this. I'll send Darren for a mop."

She made a magic circle with her wand, but, instead of saying "Darren Grimm mop up the mess," she got a little bit muddled and said, "Darren Grimm mess up the mop."

Darren grinned and rushed off to the kitchen. He came back with a mop and a large pair of scissors and gave the mop a haircut.

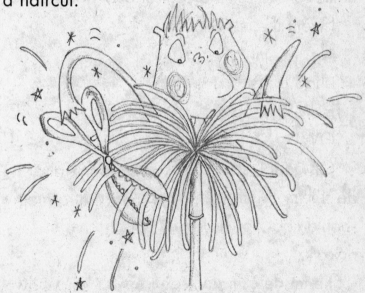

"What are you doing? Stop that this minute," yelled his mum. "That's my best mop."

"I need a cup of tea," said Grandma, and shuffled into the kitchen.

"Me too," muttered Dad. "Crazy kids!"

Airy Fairy shook her head. "Still nothing out of ten for spelling, Airy Fairy," she muttered.

It got worse.

The twins switched on the telly and the battle for the remote control broke out.

"I want the remote."

"No, I want it."

"I had it first."

THUMP.

"OW!"

"Oh dear," said Airy Fairy. "This won't do. I'll try another of my spells. I think Dawn should cool down. I think I'll send her for a walk."

She made a magic square with her wand and started writing in the air. But her spelling wasn't very good and, instead of sending Dawn for a walk she sent her for a wok.

Dawn disappeared into the kitchen and came back with a frying pan and a wooden spoon and clanged them together in everyone's ears.

"Oh dear," sighed Airy Fairy, trying to cover her own ears. "Still nothing out of ten for spelling, and I was sure I'd got that one right, too."

She was just going over the spell again in her head when a tiny movement at the window caught her eye. She looked over, and there was Scary Fairy making a horrible face at her. Airy Fairy got such a fright she nearly fell off the tree.

"Now what is she doing here?" she muttered. "She should be in school getting the hall ready for tonight's party. I bet she's come to cause more trouble."

She had. Scary Fairy wiggled her wand and suddenly Airy Fairy was covered in spots. Big red shiny spots, which itched.

It didn't take long for the Grimm family to spot her.

"That tree fairy's got spots on her face," said Mum. "I don't remember them being there before."

"I hope they're not catching," wheezed Grandma. "I'm an old lady. I don't want to catch any horrible diseases."

"I'll throw the fairy in the bin," said Dad, and headed towards the tree.

"Oh no," Airy Fairy thought aloud. "I can't let them throw me in the bin. I'll never be able to do my good fairy magic if I'm in the bin. I must do a spell to stop them talking about me."

She made a magic figure of eight with her wand and she meant to say, "Please stop the Grimms talking," but she was still thinking about Dawn and said, "Please stop the Grimms walking."

"Hey, what's happened?" cried Dad, suddenly halting two feet from the tree. "My legs have gone funny. I can't move."

"Me neither," said Mum, trying to stand up.

"Or us," said the twins, falling over on to the carpet.

"Huh," said Grandma, not getting up from the sofa. "Serves you right. Now you know what it's like. I've had bad legs for years, but I didn't get any sympathy from you lot."

"Oh no," muttered Airy Fairy. "Now what have I done? I've made things even worse."

She was just having a worry nibble at her bottom lip when –

PING! The branch below her creaked and Fairy Gropplethorpe appeared in front of her.

She looked at Airy Fairy and shook her head.

"You've used up three of your spells already, Airy Fairy," she said, "and the Grimms are no better. And look at you, covered in spots, though that's not your fault. I'll deal with that person later, and I'll help you out just this once."

And she whisked her wand in a zigzag fashion and removed the spots from Airy Fairy, and the memory of what had happened from the Grimms.

"Now concentrate, Airy Fairy," she whispered before she disappeared. "Remember you only have three spells left to do some good fairy magic to improve the Grimms – or no Christmas party!"

Chapter Four

Christmas morning came early in the Grimm house. Airy Fairy felt she had hardly gone to sleep when the sitting room door banged open and the twins, still in their pyjamas, charged in. Mum, Dad and Grandma followed more slowly, scratching and yawning. Darren and Dawn made straight for the Christmas tree. It shivered and shook as they grabbed their presents from underneath. Airy Fairy held on tight as they began ripping off the wrapping paper.

"Yuck, what horrible jumpers," muttered the twins, as they unwrapped stripy, multicoloured sweaters. "We wouldn't be seen dead in those!" And they dropped them on the floor among the wrapping paper.

Airy Fairy gulped and looked at Grandma. Her face was like a stormy thundercloud.

"Ungrateful little brats," she muttered. "It took me a long time to knit those jumpers, with the arthritis in my old fingers."

The twins just shrugged.

Mum and Dad picked up their present from Darren and Dawn and shook it.

"What do you think it is?" Mum asked Dad. "It doesn't look very interesting, and it's a very odd shape."

"Dunno," muttered Dad, and gave it a poke. "It feels a bit lumpy and bumpy."

Airy Fairy drew in her breath and looked at the twins. Their brows were lowered and their mouths were turned down.

"We made that for you in school," they said. "It's a bowl for keeping sweets in. It's made out of papier mâché, and it took us ages to tear the paper up into tiny bits."

"Really," yawned Mum and Dad.

Grandma poked at the family's present to her with her stick.

"That parcel's soft and squashy," she said.
"I hope it's not another pair of pink
bedsocks. You always buy me pink
bedsocks. I've got millions of them. I asked
for a giant box of soft-centred chocolates.
Why don't you listen? Why didn't you buy
me those!"

Airy Fairy looked all round the family.
None of them were happy. Their faces were
nearly as mean as Scary Fairy's.

Oh dear, she thought. *This isn't a very
good start to Christmas. Everyone's supposed
to be jolly at this time of year. Perhaps I
could do a little spell to make them all say
they were only joking about the presents.
Perhaps they could say something nice.*

She waved her little wand in a magic
diamond and wrote in the air, "Make the
Grimms say something nice." And she was
trying so hard to get it right that she didn't
notice Scary Fairy at the window using her
wand to rewrite the spell so that it said,

"Make the Grimms bring on some mice." And instead of the family saying something nice, they all yelled "MICE!" Suddenly, there were mice everywhere. On the carpet, on the table, on Grandma's head. She tried to fend them off with her stick. "Get off me. Get off!"

There were mice under the chairs, under the sofa, under Mum's feet. She did a funny little dance to avoid them. "Go away. Go away!"

The mice ran up the wall, up the curtains, up Dad's trouser leg. He went bananas! "Get down. Get down!"

The mice scurried over the dog, over the cat, over the hamster's cage. The dog barked and pranced about, the cat miaowed and jumped up on Mum, the hamster trembled, shot back into his bed and pulled the cotton wool in after him.

Everyone was yelling and screaming and leaping about. The presents were trampled, the Christmas tree was knocked over and Airy Fairy crashed to the floor.

"Help," she yelled, but nobody heard the tiny fairy voice amid all the din.

Airy Fairy struggled to her feet, parted the Christmas tree branches, and peeped out. What a mess! Then she caught sight of the face at the window, laughing fit to burst. Scary Fairy! This was all her doing! Scary Fairy made a horrible face at Airy Fairy and disappeared.

"Scary Fairy's up to her usual tricks," muttered Airy Fairy. "Now I'll have to use up another of my spells to get rid of the mice."

Airy Fairy made another magic diamond in the air and said, "Mice, mice, disappear. Your presence isn't wanted here." This time the spell worked, and the mice disappeared as quickly as they had come.

The Grimm family stopped yelling and jumping around and looked suspiciously at each other.

"There's something very strange going on here," they all muttered, as they righted the Christmas tree, and stuck Airy Fairy back on the top. "Where did all these mice come from? Who brought them into the house?"

Nobody owned up.

"Was it your idea of a joke?" Mum and Dad asked the twins. "Have you got a box full of mice somewhere?"

The twins shook their heads. "We don't like mice. Bet they belong to Grandma. Bet she brought them in to put in that terrible stew she makes."

"I think it was you two, you horrible little toads," said Grandma. "You did it just to scare the life out of a poor old woman." And she waved her stick at them.

The Grimm family glowered at each other. Airy Fairy sighed. "Help," she muttered. "I haven't managed to do any good fairy magic to improve the Grimm family. They're worse then ever. Scary Fairy is out to ruin my chances of getting to the school Christmas party, and I've only got one spell left. What am I going to do?"

Chapter Five

Airy Fairy stood at the top of the tree and thought and thought. How could she use the one spell that she had left to sort out Scary Fairy and the Grimms?

She was so busy thinking she hardly noticed when the Grimms sat down to lunch. She hardly noticed when the twins had a Brussel sprout battle. She hardly noticed when Grandma took out her teeth to chew her turkey.

She hardly noticed when Mum and Dad
and the twins started to scoff a large box of
soft-centred chocolates that should have been
for Grandma.

But she did notice a little cord hanging by
the side of the window.

"That's the cord I swung on earlier," she
said. "I bet it closes the curtains. If I could
just get over there and pull the curtains shut,
Scary Fairy wouldn't be able to see in to do
any of her mischief. Then, perhaps, I could
try to do some good fairy magic with my last
spell. But I mustn't be seen."

She waited and waited till it was getting dark.

Perhaps the Grimms will close the curtains themselves, she thought, but they didn't. They were too busy fighting about what to watch on TV.

"We want to watch the cartoons," said the twins.

"I want to watch a game show," said Mum.

"I want to watch some sport," said Dad.

"I want to watch an old movie," said Grandma.

While they were arguing Airy Fairy saw her chance. She slid down from the topmost spiky branch. "Ow, rotten pine needles!" she muttered, and tiptoed along the branch nearest the window. So far so good. She glanced back over her shoulder at the Grimms. They were slouched on the sofa. Darren was sucking his thumb, Dawn was fiddling with her hair, Mum and Dad were still cramming in chocolates faster than you could say "GREAT BIG GREEDY GUTS!", and Grandma was starting to snore.

Airy Fairy reached the end of the branch. It bent downwards slightly and a red shiny bauble slid off and bounced on the carpet. Airy Fairy froze and held her breath. But no one had noticed. She stretched out to grab the curtain cord, but it was just out of reach.

"I wonder if I should try out my wings again," she muttered. "I wonder if I could fly across."

But before she could take off a hand shot out and grabbed her.

"Stupid fairy's fallen off the top of the tree," Darren said, and plonked her back on the topmost spiky branch.

Oh no, Airy Fairy thought, standing there with a frozen smile on her face. *Now what am I going to do?*

She waited till the Grimms were all fighting over a board game.

"I want to be first to start," said Darren.

"No, me," said Dawn. "I'm twenty-five minutes older than you."

"Then we'll be first," smirked Mum and Dad. "We're twenty-five years older than you."

"Then I'll be first," cackled Grandma. "I'm the oldest of the lot of you." And she grabbed the dice and threw a six.

Airy Fairy saw her chance. She gritted her teeth and slid down the tree on her bottom till she reached the part where the branches were thickest.

"I'll just trek through this jungle till I reach the curtains," she gasped. But she parted a branch and – "We wish you a merry Christmas. We wish you a merry Christmas..." She had trodden on the wobbly red Santa.

"How did that happen?" said Dawn. "There's nobody near the tree." And she went over to look. She found Airy Fairy standing there with her smile stuck on, and pine needles sticking out of her hair and her frock.

"That stupid fairy's fallen off the top branch again," she said, plonking her back. "You would think she was alive and could go walkabout or something."

Airy Fairy stood there staring straight ahead, not daring to move.

"What am I going to do?" she worried. "What am I going to do?"

To make matters worse, the Christmas tree lights started to blink. On-off. On-off. On-off. Some Christmas tree lights are supposed to blink, but not the Grimms'.

"What's wrong with the lights?"
said Darren, and
came over to give
the tree a
shake.

Airy Fairy held on tight.

"Probably just need a thump," said Dawn,
and gave the tree a bigger shake.

Airy Fairy held on tighter.

The lights went out and stayed out.

Darren and Dawn shook the tree till Airy
Fairy's head was spinning and she was sure
she was going to fall off. Then, out of the
corner of her eye she caught sight of a little
light outside the window. It came from the
end of Scary Fairy's wand. She was heading
this way.

Airy Fairy was desperate. But the shaking tree gave her an idea. When the tree swung nearest the curtain, she clung on with her knees, reached out and pulled the curtain cord with all her might. The curtains slid shut, and there was so much commotion with the tree, nobody noticed.

But Airy Fairy noticed the angry expression on Scary Fairy's face just as the curtains closed, and heard the tiny tapping as she banged furiously on the window with her wand.

"That's sorted you out," grinned Airy Fairy.

The twins finally gave up shaking the tree and started feeding mince pies to the dog. He was promptly sick over Grandma's slippers.

Grandma kicked off her slippers and they landed on the cat.

He ran up the curtains and sat quivering on top of the curtain pole.

Mum looked over at him and frowned.

"Who closed these curtains?" she said. "You know I like to be able to look out to see what the neighbours are up to."

Oh no, thought Airy Fairy. *She's going to open the curtains. Scary Fairy will be able to do her worst again, after all my hard work. I'll have to do my last spell right now.*

And she screwed up her eyes, waved her little wand in a double circle and said,

"Please allow the family Grimm
To let the Christmas spirit in.
Grandma, parents, sister, brother.
Make them kinder to each other."

Airy Fairy opened her eyes and looked round. Nothing happened. There was silence.

"Oh no, Airy Fairy," she groaned. "Nothing out of ten for magic again. I'll never get to the Christmas party now!"

Then a wonderful thing took place.

"On second thoughts," said Mum. "I think I'll leave the curtains closed. It's cosier that way. Now would you like some soft-centred chocolates, Grandma? I bought them for everybody."

"Put them into that nice bowl the twins made us for Christmas," said Dad. "Weren't they clever."

"But not as clever as Grandma knitting us these super sweaters," said the twins. "They'll be great for when we go skateboarding in the park."

66

"Oh, you wouldn't catch me skateboarding,"
laughed Grandma. "I'll keep my feet firmly on
the ground in my new pink bedsocks."

Airy Fairy couldn't believe her ears. Her
last spell had actually worked. The Grimms
were being nice to each other.

She smiled happily to herself. "That's better,
Airy Fairy," she said. "One out of ten for magic."

"Oh, more than that, Airy Fairy," said a
voice, as a branch creaked behind her and
Fairy Gropplethorpe appeared.
"Much more than that. You
did very well indeed,
despite certain
people trying
to hinder
you."

Airy Fairy smiled but said nothing.
Nobody likes a tell-tale.

"Now come along," said Fairy
Gropplethorpe. "Your job here is done. It's
time to go back to school and get ready for
the party." And she waved her wand and
whisked them both away.

Chapter Six

Fairy Gropplethorpe's Academy was ready for the Christmas party. The fairies had been busy all afternoon decorating the school hall. Buttercup had painted glittering silver stars on the windows, while Tingle had twisted shiny silver string into garlands that wove their way round the walls. Tiny bunches of miniature holly sat in hazelnut-shell bowls on the window ledges, and trails of ivy hung from the lights.

Airy Fairy stood at the hall doorway and gazed in amazement.

Buttercup and Tingle caught sight of her. "Hooray, you're back," they cried and ran to give her a hug.

"You've all worked so hard," said Airy Fairy. "The hall is beautiful."

"Well, most of us have worked hard," muttered Tingle. "Some people kept disappearing all afternoon." And she looked over at Scary Fairy who was scowling in a corner.

Airy Fairy said nothing.

"So what happened, Airy Fairy?" asked Buttercup. "How did you get on? Were the Grimms really awful?"

"They were," said Airy Fairy, "but I managed to do some good fairy magic in the end. Fairy Gropplethorpe was really pleased, so she brought me back in time for the party. We rode part of the way on a red squirrel. He was a handsome fellow and very polite. His red bushy tail tickled my cheek all the way home."

"Oh, red squirrels are my favourite," sighed Tingle.

Scary Fairy scowled even more when she heard this. Red squirrels were everybody's favourite.

The door of the hall opened and Miss
Stickler came in, followed by Fairy
Gropplethorpe and Macduff. Macduff
panted over to greet Airy Fairy and rubbed
his great head on her grubby pink frock.

"Hullo, Macduff," smiled Airy Fairy. "Why
aren't you ready for the party?" And without
thinking, she raised her little wand and
magicked him up a handsome
red collar with a silver bell.

"There," she said, fastening it on. "You
look very smart."

"Which is more than can be said for you,
Airy Fairy," said Miss Stickler. "You can't go
to the party looking like that, and we're
about to play the first game. Go upstairs and
get changed right away."

Airy Fairy flew upstairs.

"Hooray," she cried. "My wings are
working again." And she dived into her
bedroom, caught her wings in the door, and
bent them all over again.

"Oops!"

She splashed her face with water from the tap and changed into her favourite jeans and a T-shirt.

"Now I'm ready to party," she said, and sat on the bannister and slid all the way back down to the hall. It was a pity she'd forgotten the knob at the end of the bannister was missing.

It was a pity the fairies and Miss Stickler were all lined up for a game of musical bumps. It was a pity Airy Fairy crashed right into them and knocked them all over.

"Airy Fairy," yelled Miss Stickler. "What are you doing? I never met such a girl for messing things up. Get into line immediately."

"Yes, Miss Stickler," grinned Airy Fairy, and looked around. "But there are only nine of us here," she said. "Where's Scary Fairy? Isn't she playing this game too?"

"No," said Miss Stickler. "Fairy Gropplethorpe said since the Grimm family no longer had a fairy at the top of their tree someone else should go and be there. Scary Fairy very kindly volunteered. Wasn't that good of her? Especially since she seems to have mislaid her wand and can't do any fairy magic."

"Oh yes, it's very good of her," said Airy Fairy, and looked at Fairy Gropplethorpe.

Fairy Gropplethorpe looked back, and Airy Fairy was almost sure she gave her a wink.

Fairy Gropplethorpe switched on the music and started to dance. "Let's party, Fairies!" she said.

Airy Fairy grinned happily. "No problem, Fairy Gropplethorpe. I can get ten out of ten for that!"

Airy Fairy

Magic Muddle!

For Lucy Charlotte,
with love

Chapter One

It was the start of a new term at Fairy Gropplethorpe's Academy for Good Fairies. Airy Fairy sighed as she pulled on her pink school frock and her pink fairy shoes.

She loved living at Fairy Gropplethorpe's Academy with the other nine little orphan fairies. She loved the Christmas holidays at school, with all the party games and delicious food, but now it was back to difficult lessons.

Airy Fairy trailed out of her bedroom and looked down over the bannister into the big school hall. All the decorations had been taken down, and the hall looked a bit bare.

"I wish we could have holidays all the time," she said to her best friends, Buttercup and Tingle. "I like holidays. I could get ten out of ten for holidays. I'm good at holidays."

"You're not much good at anything else,"
sneered Scary Fairy, coming downstairs
behind Airy Fairy and poking her with her
wand. "Bet you don't get
anything right this
term. Again."

"Just ignore her, Airy Fairy," said Buttercup
and Tingle, "she's a pain."

But it was very difficult to ignore Scary Fairy.
She was clever and sly. She was always
picking on Airy Fairy, but Airy Fairy was
always the one who got caught. Especially by
Miss Stickler, their teacher. Scary Fairy
was Miss Stickler's niece and Miss Stickler
thought she could do nothing wrong. She also

thought Airy Fairy could do nothing right.

Airy Fairy sighed again. What a pity the holidays had to end.

Airy Fairy and her friends took their seats at the front of the hall and waited for assembly to begin. As usual Scary Fairy slid in behind them. They stood up when Fairy Gropplethorpe came in, but she waved them all to sit down again.

"Good morning, Fairies," she smiled. "I'm pleased to see you all looking so bright and cheerful this morning. I expect you're eager to get back to your school work."

Not really, thought Airy Fairy, *I never seem to get any of it right. But perhaps things will be better this term. Perhaps over the holidays I'll have magically become really clever.*

She gazed out of the window and put on what she thought was a really clever expression. She screwed up her eyes and peered down her nose, but all that did was make her sneeze.

But maybe this term I will be top of the class, she thought, *and Miss Stickler and Fairy Gropplethorpe will be really pleased with me.* She could just picture herself going up on to the platform to receive a prize at the end of term for being the best fairy in the school.

It would be a really nice prize too, like an enormous box of chocolates or a picnic basket. Then she and her friends could slip down to the hall and have a midnight feast. She was just thinking about what might be in the picnic basket – cream buns, chocolate cake, fizzy pop ... when someone poked her from behind.

"Pay attention to Fairy Gropplethorpe," a voice whispered.

"Stop poking me, Scary Fairy," muttered Airy Fairy, and she reached behind her to poke Scary Fairy with her own wand.

"Airy Fairy, what ARE you doing?" said a stern voice.

"Oh no," gasped Airy Fairy, as she slowly turned.

Scary Fairy was no longer behind her. Scary Fairy had moved. In her place sat Miss Stickler. Miss Stickler had poked her to make her pay attention and Airy Fairy had just poked her back.

"Erm er, sorry, Miss Stickler," said Airy Fairy. "I thought it was … erm … er … I didn't know it was you."

Miss Stickler glared at Airy Fairy.

"Not a good start to the new term, Airy Fairy," she said. "Not a good start at all."

And it got worse.

Fairy Gropplethorpe had news for the fairies.

"I have just had a letter from Fairy Noralott, the chief inspector of schools. She is concerned about how fit we all are. She thinks that because we fairies fly everywhere we are not getting enough exercise to keep us healthy."

I don't fly everywhere, thought Airy Fairy. *My wings are usually much too wonky for me to fly anywhere.*

"So," went on Fairy Gropplethorpe. "Fairy Noralott has asked me to organize the Fairy Olympics. This will be a competition to see who is the fittest fairy in the school."

"A competition," muttered Airy Fairy to Buttercup and Tingle. "I don't like the sound of that. In a competition someone has to come last and it's sure to be me."

But Fairy Gropplethorpe hadn't finished.

"The Fairy Olympics will take place in a few weeks' time, so, I want you to concentrate on getting fit, Fairies. I want you to take lots more exercise. Spend more time in the gym, more time out of doors, and less time flying everywhere. Wings are to be folded back neatly and I want you to walk everywhere instead."

"Oh, that'll take ages," whispered
Buttercup and Tingle.

"And I've got a hole in my fairy shoes,"
sighed Airy Fairy. "Still, at least we're not
going to have extra spelling homework, or
flying backwards lessons. I still bump into
things flying forwards."

"One more thing," said
Fairy Gropplethorpe.

"Fairy Noralott will be handing out a special prize at the Fairy Olympics for the best fairy in the competition. I wonder who will win it. You will all try really hard, Fairies, won't you?"

"Oh yes, Fairy Gropplethorpe," chorused the fairies.

"Oh help," said Airy Fairy. "I'm sure to be hopeless. I'm sure to get things wrong. I don't know my left from my right or my up from my down. I'm sure to get in a muddle."

"Stop worrying, Airy Fairy," said Buttercup and Tingle. "You'll be fine."

"No, you won't," muttered Scary Fairy to herself. "I'll get the special prize. You'll get everything all wrong as usual. I'll see to that."

Chapter Two

The fitness programme began right away. Miss Stickler sent all the fairies to change into their PE kit, then led them all to the gym.

"Right, Fairies," she said. "We've no time to waste. We'll start off with an exercise to warm us up. I want you to run round the gym in a clockwise direction. Begin." And she blew her little silver whistle. *PEEEEP!*

"Oh, I can run round the gym," said Airy Fairy. "Anyone can do that. Perhaps this won't be so bad after all." And she led the way.

Then she noticed the laces on her pink fairy trainers were loose. *That could cause an accident,* she thought, and bent down to tie them. Nine fairies crashed into her and fell over in a heap. *HELP!*

They all unscrambled themselves and stood up and rubbed their bumps and bruises. Airy

Fairy emerged rather dazed from the bottom of the heap.

"What an idiot you are!" Scary Fairy scowled. "You can't even run round the gym without causing accidents!"

Miss Stickler raised her eyes heavenwards. "Do try to be careful, Airy Fairy," she said.

"Yes, Miss Stickler. Sorry, Miss Stickler," said Airy Fairy.

"Right, Fairies," went on Miss Stickler. "Hopping on one foot now. Start with the right foot. Begin." And she blew her little silver whistle.

PEEEEP!

Airy Fairy paid close attention and copied exactly what Miss Stickler did.

But she was standing opposite Miss Stickler.

"You're hopping on the wrong foot, Airy Fairy," said her teacher.

"No, I'm hopping on the right foot," said Airy Fairy.

The other fairies giggled. Airy Fairy was
always so funny.

"Change to the left foot, Fairies," called
Miss Stickler.

Airy Fairy got a bit muddled. *If my right
foot's my wrong foot, will my left foot be my
right foot?* she wondered.

"I know," she said. "I'll just hop from one

foot to the other. That way I'm bound to be right some of the time. Or left."

Miss Stickler shook her head when she saw her. "Do stop being an idiot, Airy Fairy," she said.

Airy Fairy sighed
and blew out
her cheeks.
No matter how
hard she tried
she was always
in trouble.

"Now, Fairies," Miss Stickler went on. "We'll move on to climbing up the ropes. Find a partner. One fairy at the bottom of the rope to keep it steady while the other climbs up. Begin."

Airy Fairy looked round for Buttercup or Tingle, but before she could partner them, Scary Fairy rushed over. "I'll be your partner, Airy Fairy," she said. "You go first."

Airy Fairy reluctantly agreed and looked at

the rope. It went a long way up to the ceiling. It would be so much easier just to fly, but Fairy Gropplethorpe had said wings had to be neatly folded back. Airy Fairy glanced back at her wings. They weren't exactly neatly folded. More like really squashed, with bits of sticking plaster on them from when she'd caught them in her bedroom door.

"Oh well." Airy Fairy caught hold of the end of the rope and began the long climb to the top. It was hard work and her face was as pink as her gym shorts when she got there. But it was worth it. There was a really good view from the window. Airy Fairy could see the branches of the oak tree which surrounded the school. It just looked like an abandoned tree house to human beings. Airy Fairy could also see a red squirrel. He had come out to warm himself in the winter sunshine, and was sitting on a branch nibbling a nut. The sunlight glinted through his red bushy tail, and his bright little eyes winked at Airy Fairy.

"Oh, he's lovely," she breathed. She was so busy admiring the squirrel she didn't see Scary Fairy give the rope a sharp tug.

"Help," cried Airy Fairy as she lost her grip. She grabbed for the rope but it slipped through her fingers.

Aaaaaaaargh.

Wheeee.

Whump. She landed on Miss Stickler's head, sending her crashing to the floor.

"Airy Fairy," yelled Miss Stickler, who had put her knee through her stocking and bent her whistle in the fall. "What DO you think you're doing?"

"Nothing. I mean, sorry, Miss Stickler," gasped Airy Fairy, her legs in the air and her wings more bent than ever. "I fell off. I mean the rope moved. I mean I saw the squirrel then... I mean... Sorry, Miss Stickler."

Scary Fairy hurried over.

"I was holding the rope perfectly still, Aunt Stickler," she lied. "Airy Fairy is just so careless. I do hope you haven't hurt your head. Lean on me and I'll help you back to the classroom."

"Thank you, Scary Fairy. You're very kind. I think we should all go back to the classroom before there are any more mishaps."

99

Buttercup and Tingle were sympathetic as Airy Fairy trailed back to the classroom. "Scary Fairy must have yanked the rope," they said.

"But Miss Stickler will never believe that," muttered Airy Fairy and looked on miserably as Scary Fairy insisted on putting a bandage on Miss Stickler's head.

She had just finished tying it when Fairy Gropplethorpe came into the classroom.

"Well, how did the first fitness lesson go?" she beamed. Then she noticed Miss Stickler's head, and all the fairies' bumps and bruises. "Oh dear," she said. "How did that happen?"

"It was all Airy Fairy's fault," smirked Scary Fairy. "She was the cause of all the accidents."

Airy Fairy looked at her feet and scuffed the toes of her pink fairy trainers. She just knew these Fairy Olympics were going to be a complete disaster for her. Scary Fairy would make sure of that.

Chapter Three

But Fairy Gropplethorpe was determined that the fairies should get fit.

"Change back into your school frocks, Fairies," she beamed, "and come outside. I have magicked up a little surprise for you."

The fairies and Miss Stickler trooped outside and sat among the branches of the oak tree. Fairy Gropplethorpe chose a stout branch and balanced on it. It creaked loudly.

"Today," she said, "we are going down into the garden."

"Shall we fly down, Fairy Gropplethorpe?" asked Airy Fairy, leaning over to peer at the ground below. *Oops*, she leaned forward too far and fell off her branch. Tingle had to grab her by the back of her frock till she swung herself up again.

"No," said Fairy Gropplethorpe. "Wings must stay neatly folded back. We're going to climb down. The surprise is waiting for us at the bottom."

"Climb down?" gasped Airy Fairy, taking another nervous peek. The ground was a long way away.

"Yes," said Fairy Gropplethorpe. "I have magicked up a little ladder. Look."

She pointed to the side of the tree and there, snaking its way down to the ground, was a little rope ladder.

"Help," cried Airy Fairy. "I'll never get down that. I'm sure to trip over my feet or my shoelaces. I'm sure to fall off."

"Oh no, you won't," said Buttercup and Tingle.

"Oh yes, you will," muttered Scary Fairy.

"What's the surprise, Fairy Gropplethorpe?" asked Buttercup.

"You'll find out when we reach the ground," smiled the head teacher. "Now I'll lead the way. Climb down behind me, Fairies, one by one."

"You go before me," said Airy Fairy to all the other fairies. She waited until they were all safely down.

"Your turn now, Airy Fairy," said Miss Stickler. "Off you go."

Airy Fairy checked that her laces were tied and put her tiny pink trainer – her right one, or it may have been her left – on to the little rope ladder and began the long climb down. She was halfway there and was doing quite well, till she stopped to look down. Fairy Gropplethorpe and all the other fairies were on the ground and so was something else. A team of lively ponies. Fairy Gropplethorpe had magicked them up for a riding lesson.

"Oh, how lovely," said Airy Fairy. "I hope I get that little white one."

And she was so busy admiring it, she didn't see Scary Fairy at the bottom of the ladder give it a hefty push. It swung wildly from side to side. So did Airy Fairy.

"Aaaaaargh!" She tried to hang on, but she scraped her knees, her knuckles and her nose on the bark of the tree, and she let go and fell off. She went tumbling head over heels towards the ground and landed on the back of the little white pony. Facing his tail!

He got such a fright, he picked up his hooves and took off through the bushes. Airy Fairy hung on to him.

"Help, help!" she yelled. "I can't find the pony's head. Where did it go? It must be here somewhere!"

SWISH! The little white pony flicked his tail and nearly knocked her off.

Fairy Gropplethorpe and the other fairies mounted their ponies and set off in hot pursuit.

They chased Airy Fairy past the bed of winter pansies, past the rhododendron bushes and over the crisp grass, still white and sparkling from the night frost. They could see Airy Fairy had her eyes closed. They could see she was hanging on to the saddle for all she was worth. They could see the garden pond. So could the little white pony.

He gave a pleased little whinny and
stopped abruptly for a drink. *WHEEEEE!* Airy
Fairy lost her hold and sailed through the air.

WHIZZZZZ! She skated on her bottom across
the frozen pond ...

... till *SPLASH!* She landed in the icy water in the middle. *Cough, choke, splutter!* She spat out the pond water, swam to the edge of the ice, then hauled herself out.

When Fairy Gropplethorpe and the other fairies arrived she was standing at the side of the pond, sopping wet, and covered in slimy green weed.

"Oh, Airy Fairy, are you all right?" said
Fairy Gropplethorpe, taking off her cloak
and wrapping it round her. "You'll never get
to be a fit fairy at this rate."

"Huh, just look at her. She's not fit to be a
fairy," sneered Scary Fairy. "She should be a
warty toad instead."

Fairy Gropplethorpe helped Airy Fairy
back up on to the little white pony. "It helps if
you face the right way, Airy Fairy," she said,
and she took the reins and led Airy Fairy
safely back to school.

Airy Fairy climbed the long ladder back up to the Academy and, when she had changed into some warm dry clothes, went to join Miss Stickler in the classroom.

Miss Stickler had stayed behind to mark the spelling books. She had just reached Airy Fairy's when she arrived.

"Still nothing out of ten for spelling, Airy Fairy," she frowned. "You had better do some more."

Airy Fairy gave a deep sigh and took up her pencil.

"Spell bough," said Miss Stickler.

Airy Fairy wrote down *b* and stopped. "Is that bough as in tree or bow as in dog?" she asked, and, just to be helpful, she did her dog impersonation. "Bow wow. Bow wow. Ruff ruff ruff."

Miss Stickler closed her eyes and shook her head.

"Bough as in tree," she said.

"Got it," said Airy Fairy and wrote it down. *Bowgh.*

Miss Stickler looked at the word. She didn't look pleased.

Airy Fairy chewed the end of her pencil. "I haven't got it right, have I?" she said. "Sometimes I get a bit muddled."

Chapter Four

To make matters worse, later that week, Fairy Gropplethorpe had another surprise in store for the fairies.

"I have booked you all a session at the local Elf Club," she announced.

"Oh," said Airy Fairy. "Won't we all develop muscles if we go there? I don't think I want to change my name to Muscles the fairy."

"Don't be so silly, Airy Fairy," said Miss Stickler. "The Elf Club is very exclusive. It's where all the fairy pop stars go to keep fit."

"Perhaps we'll see Freddy Sprite," said Scary Fairy. "He's my favourite pop star."

"Perhaps we will," said Fairy Gropplethorpe. "But we are going there as part of our get fit campaign. Put on your warm coats and hats, Fairies, and we'll set off. No need to take your wands, you won't be doing any magic today."

Airy Fairy put on her pink fairy coat and pulled on her pink fairy hat. It was too big for her and kept falling down over her eyes and ears, so she didn't see Scary Fairy slip her wand into her coat pocket, and she didn't hear her mutter to herself, "I could do some magic at the Elf Club and muddle up Airy Fairy even more."

"Now stay in a neat line," said Fairy Gropplethorpe, when they had all got safely down the ladder from the oak tree. "Miss Stickler will lead the way and I'll bring up the rear."

"It's a chilly day, Fairies," said Miss Stickler, "so we'll march briskly to warm us up. Follow me and do what I do. Left right, left right. Swing your arms, heads up straight. Left right, left right. Lift your feet, stretch your legs. Left right, left right... Airy Fairy, what ARE you doing?"

Airy Fairy was doing a little dance in the middle of the line.

"Sorry, Miss Stickler," she panted, "I'm just catching up with the others. My hat fell over my eyes when I held my head up straight, so I couldn't see where we were going or what we were doing. But I was swinging my legs and stretching my arms. Right left, right left. Just like you said... What was it you said again?"

The other fairies grinned. They just loved Airy Fairy. She always made them laugh.

But Scary Fairy didn't laugh.

"She's a complete idiot," she muttered. "Why does everyone laugh at her? Why does everyone like her?"

"Just put one foot in front of the other and try to get to the Elf Club in one piece, Airy Fairy," sighed Miss Stickler.

The band of tiny fairies trooped down the country road, crossed where it was safe, and came to a halt in front of the Elf Club. To human beings the Elf Club just looked like a large abandoned dog kennel, half hidden by some hawthorn bushes, but inside it was Ollie's gym. Ollie was an old friend of Fairy Gropplethorpe's.

"Hullo, Henrietta, Miss Stickler, Fairies," he said. "Welcome to the Elf Club. Of course, this 'ere club's not just for elves, but for all fairy folk who wants to get fit. And Fairy Gropplethorpe tells me that's what you want to do, right?"

Not really, thought Airy Fairy, looking round her at all the fitness machines. *These machines look dangerous.*

"Now all the machines are perfectly safe," said Ollie, as if reading Airy Fairy's mind. "I'll show you how they work."

"Bet you still get them in a muddle, Airy Fairy," smirked Scary Fairy, giving her a sly pinch.

"Take no notice of her," said Buttercup and Tingle and put their arms round Airy Fairy.

Ollie explained how everything worked and the fairies got started.

Buttercup had a go on the rowing machine.

"Row, row, row your boat gently down the stream," she sang, as she rowed away to nowhere.

"This is fun," she said to Airy Fairy. "Why don't you have a go?"

It looked safe enough, but Airy Fairy wasn't keen.

Tingle tried out one of the weights machine.

"Wait a minute," cried Airy Fairy. "Are you sure that's not too heavy?"

"Oh no, it's fun," puffed Tingle. "Why don't you have a go?"

It looked safe enough, but Airy Fairy wasn't keen.

Then Miss Stickler came over.

"Why are you standing about doing nothing, Airy Fairy?" she said. "Choose a machine and get on with it. You'll never get fit at this rate."

Airy Fairy looked around. Buttercup and Tingle had swapped places and all the rest of the fairies were scattered around the room. She couldn't see Scary Fairy, but she did spy an empty walking machine. The one opposite was occupied by someone wearing sunglasses and purple shorts. And he was walking, walking, walking...

"I'll try the walking machine," she said to Miss Stickler. "That looks safe enough."

Airy Fairy stepped on and Ollie came over and set the machine to a comfortable walking pace.

"You'll be fine with that," he smiled. "See you in a bit."

Airy Fairy walked and walked.

"This is all right," she said, "but I wish I was going somewhere."

She looked at the man opposite. He was listening to his headphones.

"That's a good idea," said Airy Fairy. "This is a bit boring."

But no sooner had she said that than her machine speeded up, and she had to walk very fast to keep up. She panted and puffed and her cheeks became hot and very red.

Then the machine speeded up again and again and Airy Fairy had to run faster and faster and faster.

"Help," she yelled, as her little legs windmilled and her hair flew out behind her. Then, just as she thought she could go on no longer, the machine went *BANG*, stopped suddenly and pitched her forward.

The man in the machine opposite caught her as *WHEEE* she shot through the air.

"Hey, slow down, little fairy," he said. "What happened to you? What happened to your machine? It's got smoke coming from it."

"I don't know," gasped Airy Fairy. "It just went faster and faster. My legs couldn't keep up."

"Well, let's take a look," said the man, and took her hand.

Ollie came running over with all the others.

"I don't understand it," he said, scratching his bald head. "That's never happened before, and I checked this machine myself."

"Well, this little fairy's tired out now," said the man, "so, she and I will go and have a glass of juice in the cafe, while you find out what went wrong. What's your name, by the way, little fairy? Mine's Freddy. Freddy Sprite." And he took off his sunglasses and held out his hand.

"The famous pop star," gasped Airy Fairy. "WOW! I'm Fairy Airy. I mean Airy Fairy. From Fairy Gropplethorpe's Academy for Good Fairies."

Freddy Sprite grinned. "Pleasure to meet you, Airy Fairy," he said. "Come and tell me all about your school. I was hopeless at school. I never got anything right."

"Me neither," grinned Airy Fairy, and they went off together chatting like old friends. All the other fairies clapped and cheered and talked excitedly about Airy Fairy meeting Freddy Sprite. All except one. Scary Fairy had a really horrible expression on her face as Airy Fairy passed by, and Airy Fairy could see, sticking out of the back of Scary Fairy's shorts, her little fairy wand.

"We were supposed to leave our wands behind," she muttered. Then she thought, *Oh no, I bet that machine didn't go bang by itself. I bet Scary Fairy's been up to her tricks again. And now that I'm chatting to her favourite pop star, she's going to be worse than ever.*

Chapter Five

At the next assembly, Fairy Gropplethorpe
had an exciting announcement.

"Good news, Fairies," she beamed. "I had
a phone call from Freddy Sprite this morning.
He's very interested in keeping fit, and in our
Fairy Olympics, so he's going to drop in on
the day to cheer us on. Isn't that splendid?"

"Ooh yes," said the Fairies.

"Oh no," said Airy Fairy. "I'm sure to be
last. I wish I hadn't told him about it now."

"Stop worrying and just try as hard as you can," said Tingle and Buttercup.

"You're right," said Airy Fairy. "I'll try really hard. Maybe I'll be all right."

"You haven't a hope," muttered Scary Fairy behind her. "You're always in a muddle." And she sneakily loosened the belt on Airy Fairy's school frock and tied it to the back of her chair.

Fairy Gropplethorpe finished her list of assembly announcements and the fairies stood up to go. Airy Fairy's chair came too. She swung it round and clunked two fairies on the knee before the chair pulled her over backwards, leaving her stranded with her pink fairy trainers in the air.

"What ARE you doing now, Airy Fairy?" asked Miss Stickler.

"Nothing, Miss Stickler," said Airy Fairy, struggling to untie her frock. "Sorry, Miss Stickler. I got a bit tangled up."

Miss Stickler shook her head and gathered all the fairies together in a corner of the hall.

"Today," she said, looking at her timetable, "we are going to do cross-country running. We are going to climb down into the garden and, starting at the holly bush, run round the rhododendron bed, past the rose garden to the finishing line at the cabbage patch on the far side."

"Run all that way," gasped Airy Fairy, "but it's metres and metres. I'm sure to get lost. I won't be back until tomorrow."

"Nonsense," said Miss Stickler. "All fairies to report back in time for lunch. Now go and get changed into your numbered running vests and shorts."

"I'll never be able to do this," said Airy Fairy later to Tingle and Buttercup as she closed her eyes to climb down the little rope ladder into the garden. "The garden's very overgrown. I'll never find my way back."

"Yes, you will," said Tingle. "Look, follow me. I'm number 8. Keep number 8 in front of you and you'll be fine."

"Good idea, Tingle," said Airy Fairy, cheering up.

"That is a good idea," muttered Scary Fairy, who'd been listening. "I know how I can muddle up Airy Fairy even more now."

All the fairies lined up by the holly bush.

"On your marks, get set, go!" said Miss Stickler.

Airy Fairy set off. She kept right behind Tingle, keeping the number 8 in sight.

They went down the long straight path that led from the holly bush to the rhododendron bed. That's when things got tricky. The rhododendrons had grown tall and fat over the years and creeping ivy had grown round their lower stems. It sent out snaky tendrils to trip up unwary fairies. Airy Fairy was so busy keeping her eye on Tingle that her ankles got snarled up in the ivy and she fell over and bumped her head on a rhododendron root.

"Ow," she said, and sat for a moment or
two rubbing her head.

That gave Scary Fairy her chance. She
picked up a muddy stone and changed the 3
on her back to an 8. Then she ran in front of
Airy Fairy.

Airy Fairy looked up. "Oh good," she
said. "I can still see the number 8," and she
set off after Scary Fairy.

Scary Fairy smiled and led her off the path, deeper and deeper into the rhododendron jungle, and further away from the rose garden. It got darker and darker as the rhododendrons closed in overhead.

"Surely we must be getting near the rose garden by now," panted Airy Fairy, and called, "Tingle, Tingle, wait for me."

But Scary Fairy ran on, and hid behind a large leaf. She waited for Airy Fairy to go past, then she headed back to the rose garden.

Airy Fairy ran round in circles. A green
frog leapt out at her and gave her a fright.
A large beetle vroomed across her path
and nearly knocked her over, and a huge
crow picked her up in his beak thinking she
might be a worm.
He deposited her
in a muddy
puddle when
he discovered
she wasn't.

Airy Fairy ran on. It began to rain. Great
fat rain drops slid down shiny green leaves
on to her head. Soon she was cold and wet
and completely lost.

"Help," she called. "Help. Where is
everyone?"

There was no reply.

Airy Fairy didn't know which way to go.

"Left or right," she said. "Which way is the
rose garden?"

She had no idea.

"Perhaps if I climb up to the top of that tall rhododendron bush, I'll be able to see."

She climbed all the way up, slipping and sliding and grazing her knees. But, when she got to the top, all she could see were the other rhododendron bushes.

"Oh no," cried Airy Fairy. "How am I going to get out of here? I can't do any magic because I've no fairy wand, and I can't fly because my wings are wonky. Perhaps I'm going to be lost here for ever and ever."

Chapter Six

Airy Fairy climbed back down the rhododendron bush and sat down on a big stone to have a think. *CLUNK!* Something hit her on the head.

"What was that?" she said, and picked it up.

It was a pine nut.

"Where did that come from?" she wondered. "I don't see any pine trees."

She looked round and there, sitting high up
in the rhododendron bush, was the red
squirrel she'd seen earlier.

"Hullo, Mr Squirrel," she called. "Can
you help me? I'm looking for the rose garden
and I'm lost."

The red squirrel swung easily to the ground
and crouched down to let Airy Fairy climb
on his back. Then he set off. Airy Fairy clung
on tight to his tufty ears. Sometimes they
travelled over the ground. Sometimes through
the air.

The red squirrel brought Airy Fairy out, not at the rose garden, but at the cabbage patch. Most of the other fairies were there already and cheered as Airy Fairy slid off his back at the finishing line.

"Oh, you are lucky, Airy Fairy," said Buttercup. "Imagine getting a ride on a red squirrel. He was lovely."

"But where did you get to, Airy Fairy?" asked Tingle. "I thought you were following me."

"I was," said Airy Fairy, and told them what had happened.

"How awful," said Buttercup. "You could have been lost for days."

"Or weeks," said Tingle.

They were just about to head back to school for lunch when Scary Fairy appeared.

She stopped short in surprise.

"How did you get here before me?" she asked Airy Fairy. "I thought you were..."

"Thought she was where, Scary Fairy?" asked Tingle.

"Nowhere," muttered Scary Fairy, and turned and ran back to school, but not before the friends had noticed how muddy the number on her back was.

"Almost as though she'd changed the number then tried to rub it out again," said Buttercup.

"You mean she led Airy Fairy into the rhododendron jungle," said Tingle.

Buttercup nodded.

"Oh no," said Airy Fairy. "As if these Fairy Olympics weren't bad enough, I've got Scary Fairy's rotten tricks to worry about as well."

Chapter Seven

The day of the Fairy Olympics arrived, and all the fairies were up early to greet their guests.

"Put on your best school frocks," Fairy Gropplethorpe had instructed the fairies, "and remember to smile nicely and be polite."

But Airy Fairy couldn't find her best school frock.

"I had it on over the holidays when we all went out to tea with Mr and Mrs Goblin and all the little Goblins, but I don't know where it went after that ... oh yes I do!"

And she dived under her bed and found it
in among the apple cores and sweet
wrappers. Her best
frock was in a
terrible state.
One of the little
goblins had
covered it in
jam when he'd
sat on her knee.

"Oh well, perhaps no one will notice," said
Airy Fairy. "It's only a little bit crumpled and
sticky."

Chief Inspector Noralott arrived at the
Academy first.

"Ah, Fairy Gropplethorpe," she said. "How
nice to see you. Your fairies are looking very
smart. Well, most of them," she added,
spying Airy Fairy's sticky frock.

Airy Fairy tried to cover up the jam stain
with her hand.

"Let me introduce you to the fairies, Chief Inspector Noralott," said Miss Stickler. "This is my niece, Scary Fairy. She's our best student. And this, I'm afraid, is Airy Fairy, who's not."

Suddenly there was a flapping noise overhead and a large sparrowhawk circled the oak tree. He went round and round in ever decreasing circles, fixing them all with his yellow eye, till a figure dropped neatly from his back, and made a perfect landing on a sturdy bough. Freddy Sprite had arrived. The sparrowhawk swooped away as Freddy waved his thanks.

"Morning all," he turned to grin at
everyone. "I told you I would drop in on the
Fairy Olympics. And I've brought an extra
special prize with me. I think you'll like it, so
good luck to all of you."

The fairies went to change into their track
suits, then they all climbed down into the
garden. The grown ups took their places
inside the upturned orange box the fairies
had made into a spectator stand and the
Fairy Olympics began.

First there was the ten-metre sprint held right
in front of the spectator stand. Airy Fairy
checked that her laces were tied and took a
big deep breath.

"Try not to be last. Try not to be last," she kept muttering to herself.

READY, STEADY, GO. Miss Stickler fired the starting pistol and the fairies were off down the long gravel path. Scary Fairy elbowed her way out in front. Airy Fairy ran as fast as she could. She couldn't let Fairy Gropplethorpe down in front of Chief Inspector Noralott.

But where were the rest of her class? She could only see Scary Fairy ahead of her. She glanced behind her. There they were. She must be second in the race. But could she catch up with Scary Fairy? Then she remembered how fast she had run at the Elf Club when Scary Fairy had tampered with the walking machine. *VROOM!* Her little legs speeded up, she passed Scary Fairy, and crossed the finishing line first.

Airy Fairy couldn't believe it.
Neither could Scary Fairy.
"Where did you come from, Airy Fairy?" she hissed. "Everyone knows I'm the fastest fairy in the school."

But Fairy Gropplethorpe was jumping up and down and clapping her hands. "Well done, Airy Fairy," she called. "Very well done indeed."

"Nice one, little fairy," grinned Freddy Sprite. "Magic!"

"Was that the sticky fairy who won?" asked Chief Inspector Noralott.

Next came the pony race.

"Oh help," said Airy Fairy. "I must remember to face the right way this time."

"Bet you fall off again," muttered Scary Fairy. "I'll see to that."

But Airy Fairy heard her this time. Then she remembered how Scary Fairy had tied the belt of her frock to her chair at assembly, and she reached down and tied the laces of her trainers to the stirrups.

"I won't fall off this time," she said.

And she didn't. Not even when Scary Fairy poked the little white pony with her wand and made him rear up and gallop

faster than ever. Airy Fairy stayed on and
passed the finishing line first.

Airy Fairy couldn't believe it.
Neither could Scary Fairy.
"I don't know how you're doing it, Airy
Fairy," she said. "But I'll beat you in the
obstacle race. You're hopeless at climbing
ropes. You always fall off."
Airy Fairy gulped. She knew that was true.

The obstacle race was set up in front of the spectator stand.

This race had been Chief Inspector Noralott's idea.

"It will tell me how fit your fairies really are," she told Fairy Gropplethorpe.

There was a large climbing frame with ropes to cross, brown sacks to crawl through and a paddling pool to swim over.

Fairy Gropplethorpe wasn't keen on the race.

"At least let me put warm water in the paddling pool," she'd said. "It is winter time."

But Chief Inspector Noralott wouldn't allow it. "A little cold water never hurt anyone," she said.

The fairies lined up. Miss Stickler fired the starting pistol and they were off.

To her surprise, Airy Fairy climbed up and down the ropes with ease. This was much easier than climbing to the top of a rhododendron bush. Then she swung across the climbing frame.

Just like swinging
from the branches
of the oak tree.

Crawling through the dark brown sack was
no problem compared to the dark
rhododendron jungle, and, when she got to
the paddling pool, some of it had turned to
ice. Airy Fairy smiled, jumped on to the ice
and whizzed across it. She plunged into the
icy water in the middle.

"At least there's no pondweed in here," she spluttered as she swam quickly to the other side and hauled herself out and across the finishing line. She was too busy emptying out her trainers to hear the cheering.

She was too busy trying to get her wet hair out of her eyes to see Fairy Gropplethorpe beckoning her towards the stand.

"Go and collect your prize, Airy Fairy," whispered Tingle. "You've won the Fairy Olympics."

"What?" Airy Fairy could hardly believe it. Neither could Scary Fairy.

"How did you do it?" she muttered. "I bet you cheated."

"No, I didn't." Airy Fairy grinned. "With all your nasty tricks, you helped me practise. Thank you, Scary Fairy."

Scary Fairy made a scary face as Airy Fairy went up on to the platform to receive her prize. "Very good, Airy Fairy," said Chief Inspector Noralott, presenting her with a silver trophy. "You're the fittest fairy and a credit to Fairy Gropplethorpe's Academy."

"Well done, Airy Fairy," smiled Fairy Gropplethorpe, and she took off her cloak and wrapped it round Airy Fairy.

"You didn't slow down at all, little fairy," smiled Freddy Sprite. "I bet you're the fastest fairy in the world. Hey, that could be the title of my next hit song. Now here's the special prize I said I would present to the winner. Two tickets to my next concert."

"Oh, thank you," said Airy Fairy. Then she stopped and thought. "But I'm sorry, I can't accept them."

"Why not? Don't you like my singing?" said Freddy Sprite.

"I love it," said Airy Fairy. "But I've got more than one friend and it wouldn't be fair to choose."

"I see," Freddy Sprite was thoughtful too. "You know, Fairy Gropplethorpe," he said. "I think you have a really nice little fairy here, but my concert is a sell-out and there are no more tickets, so how about if I come to the Academy one day soon and sing to all of you."

"Oh, that would be wonderful," beamed Fairy Gropplethorpe.

"Er ... erm ... can I come too?" asked Chief Inspector Noralott.

"Everyone can come," said Airy Fairy, and held up her little silver trophy for all to see.

The fairies cheered and Airy Fairy smiled happily. She really needn't have done all that worrying. The Fairy Olympics had turned out brilliantly after all.

Airy Fairy

Magic Mess!

To Matilda, with love

Chapter One

Spring had arrived at Fairy Gropplethorpe's Academy for Good Fairies, and Miss Stickler and the fairies were decorating the school hall with the bowls of spring flowers they had grown.

"Look how pretty my snowdrops are," said Buttercup.

"Look how bright my yellow crocuses are," said Tingle.

"I don't know what's happened to mine," said Airy Fairy. "I've only got green shoots."

"You never get anything right, Airy Fairy," smirked Scary Fairy. "I bet you planted the wrong bulbs. Anyway, my bowl is easily the best. Fairy Gropplethorpe's bound to say so."

Airy Fairy sighed and took her seat for assembly. It was always the same. Scary Fairy got everything right, while she always seemed to get everything wrong. No matter how hard she tried.

When Fairy Gropplethorpe came into the hall, the ten little fairies stood up politely, but Fairy Gropplethorpe waved them back to their seats.

"Good morning, Fairies," she smiled. "It's a beautiful morning, and made all the more lovely by your spring flowers." And she stopped to admire them.

"What lovely snowdrops, Buttercup. What elegant narcissi, Cherri. And the crocuses so many of you planted are splendid, though surprisingly Scary Fairy's seem to have doubled in number," and she gave Scary Fairy a puzzled look. "I wonder how that happened?"

"Scary Fairy has green fingers," smiled Miss Stickler. Scary Fairy was her niece and Miss Stickler thought she was wonderful.

"But what's happened to this little bowl here?" said Fairy Gropplethorpe. "It has no flowers at all."

159

"That's Airy Fairy's bowl," sighed Miss Stickler. "I'm afraid she doesn't have green fingers."

Airy Fairy examined her fingers. She didn't know if she wanted them to be green, though perhaps multicoloured shiny stars on them would be nice if she was going to a party.

Fairy Gropplethorpe looked closely at Airy Fairy's bowl. "Actually Airy Fairy's bowl has done very well, it's just that she's planted spring onions instead of flowers."

The other fairies giggled. Airy Fairy always did funny things.

"Onions!" squeaked Airy Fairy. "I didn't mean to plant onions. How did that happen?" Then she remembered. Scary Fairy had handed her the bulbs to plant. This was another of her rotten tricks. She was always trying to get Airy Fairy into trouble.

"Sorry, Fairy Gropplethorpe," said Airy
Fairy. "I didn't know... I mean, I didn't
mean... I mean, sorry, Fairy Gropplethorpe."

But Fairy Gropplethorpe was smiling. "No
need to apologize, Airy Fairy. Spring onions
are very tasty, and when they're ready we
can put them into a special pie and have it
for tea. Well done."

Airy Fairy turned and made a cheeky face
at Scary Fairy. Scary Fairy scowled.

Airy Fairy really loved the springtime. She loved the way the green shoots pushed their way out of the brown earth, and she loved to watch the baby animals and birds playing in the garden.

Fairy Gropplethorpe loved the springtime too. "But there is always so much to do after the long winter," she said, "and everything outside looking so fresh and new has given me an idea. I've been looking at some of your bedrooms..."

Oh help, thought Airy Fairy. *I hope she didn't look at mine. It's a bit messy.*

But Fairy Gropplethorpe wasn't worried about tidiness. "They all look a bit uninteresting painted plain white," she said. "So, after you've finished your work in class, you can have three magic spells to paint your bedrooms any colour you wish. I have to go away to a head teachers' conference for a few days, but when I come back Miss Stickler and I will

choose the best bedroom and give this little
prize to the successful fairy." And she held
up the prettiest, daintiest fairy pen.

"Ooh," said the Fairies.

"Perhaps if I wrote with that I could get
my school work right sometimes," said
Airy Fairy.

"You've got no chance," muttered Scary Fairy, poking Airy Fairy with her wand. "I'm the cleverest fairy. I'll win that pen. Just wait and see."

"But before we think about painting or prizes, the bedrooms will have to be spring cleaned," warned Miss Stickler, who did worry about tidiness. "Some of them are very messy." And she frowned at Airy Fairy. "Very messy indeed. But you can all have three magic spells to do the cleaning."

"I'm off to my conference now," said Fairy Gropplethorpe. "Unfortunately dogs are not allowed, so please remember to look after Macduff while I'm gone. And happy painting, Fairies! I shall look forward to seeing your bright bedrooms when I return." Then away she flew.

The fairies all went back to their classroom, chatting about the news.

"I'm going to paint my room brilliant yellow," said Buttercup.

"I'm going to paint my room awesome orange," said Tingle.

"I don't know what colour to paint mine," said Airy Fairy. "I like the colour of the sea, but sometimes it's blue, sometimes it's green and sometimes it's turquoise."

"It won't matter what you do," smirked Scary Fairy. "It won't be half as good as mine. Mine is bound to be the best because I'm the best at painting and spelling. And you're the worst," she said to Airy Fairy, and poked her with her wand again.

"Oh, go and jump in a slimy swamp," said Airy Fairy, who poked her right back and was immediately caught by Miss Stickler.

"You know poking with wands is against the school rules, Airy Fairy. Lose one magic cleaning-up spell."

Airy Fairy sighed. It was always the same. She was always the one who got caught, while Scary Fairy got away with everything.

"Never mind, Airy Fairy," whispered Buttercup and Tingle. "You can easily tidy up with two spells."

Airy Fairy sat down at her desk, cupped her chin in her hands, and gazed out of the classroom window. The bright spring sun was shining on Fairy Gropplethorpe's Academy, making its windows sparkle.

To passers-by, the school just looked like an abandoned tree house, high up in an old oak, but inside it was home to ten little orphaned fairies. Airy Fairy turned her gaze to the branches of the oak tree. The oak buds were getting fat and seemed about to burst at any moment.

"I wonder why the buds never burst while I'm looking at them?" she whispered to Buttercup and Tingle. "Do you think if I gaze at them long enough, I might see them pop?" And she screwed up her eyes and gazed at them really, really hard.

"Airy Fairy, what ARE you doing?" said Miss Stickler. "Stop making silly faces at the window and get on with your work."

"Yes, Miss Stickler. Sorry, Miss Stickler. But I wasn't making silly faces, I was just trying to see the oak buds growing. Do you think they just grow when I'm not looking. Do you think if I looked away, then back again really quickly, I could catch them growing? Or do you think they just grow at night time while everyone's asleep?"

"I think you should be paying attention to your lessons instead of gazing out of the window, Airy Fairy. No wonder you're at the bottom of the class."

Behind her, Scary Fairy chanted softly, "Stupid. Stupid."

Airy Fairy sighed and picked up her pencil. She looked at the difficult sums Miss Stickler had put on the blackboard:

If it takes three fairies three days to walk three kilometres, how many days will it take them to walk nine kilometres?

Oh dear, thought Airy Fairy, sticking her pencil in her mouth and giving the end a good chew. *It's bound to take a long time. Nine kilometres is a very long way for little fairies to walk. They'll probably get blisters and not be able to walk very fast. I got a blister once and Fairy Gropplethorpe had to put a sticking plaster on my heel. And where will the fairies sleep, or will they walk all through the night as well? If they do that they'll get very tired. And hungry. I wonder if they'll stop to have something to eat, or will they take sandwiches with them? Oh, I don't know, it's all far too difficult.*

Then she had a brainwave. *Aha!* she thought. *I bet this is a trick question. Miss Stickler loves trick questions. We all know fairies don't have to walk at all.*

And she smiled and wrote down in her fairy notebook:

Answer to question one:

It would take the fairies no time at all to walk nine kilometres because they could either fly or magic themselves there immediately.

She sat back, feeling pleased with herself. She was sure that was the right answer to question one.

But it wasn't.

"Airy Fairy," sighed Miss Stickler, when she looked at Airy Fairy's notebook. "In the spring, when everything has a new beginning, I had hoped that you might begin to be more sensible too, but obviously not.

Lose one more magic cleaning-up spell for
writing silly answers, and stay behind at
break-time to do more sums."

"Oh," Airy Fairy's eyes opened wide in
surprise. "I didn't mean it to be a silly answer,
Miss Stickler. I was just so sorry for those poor
little fairies having to walk all that way..."

"It IS a long way for fairies to walk,"
nodded Cherri.

"My fairy shoes would be worn right
through," agreed Honeysuckle.

But Miss Stickler wasn't listening. Airy Fairy
gave a huge sigh. She was sure that answer
had been right, and at break-time she and
Buttercup and Tingle had planned to play
with the red squirrel.

"Never mind, Airy Fairy," whispered Buttercup. "We can see him again soon."

"And the answer to the first sum is nine days," whispered Tingle.

"You'll be nine YEARS trying to work out the answers to the rest," sneered Scary Fairy. "I always said you were an idiot. You'll never get anything right."

"Yes, I will," muttered Airy Fairy, then looked at the long row of sums she had to do. "Just maybe not today."

Chapter Two

But Airy Fairy was determined to get things right, so she concentrated really, really hard, finished all her sums, and managed to stay out of trouble all afternoon. PHEW! Then, when Miss Stickler called a special meeting after school, she put on her most intelligent expression – both eyes wide open and her tongue sticking out – and listened very carefully.

"I have called this special meeting for two reasons," said Miss Stickler. "Reason one is to remind you what you must do to make your bedrooms clean and tidy."

"I know what we must do, Aunt Stickler," volunteered Scary Fairy. "All the windows must be cleaned, the room swept and dusted, and all the rubbish thrown out. I've done it already. My bedroom is spotless."

"Well done, Scary Fairy," beamed Miss Stickler. "I knew I could count on you."

Then she looked over at Airy Fairy.

Airy Fairy was finding her intelligent expression hard to keep up, so she had tucked in her tongue and was propping open her eyelids with her fingers.

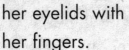

"Are you listening, Airy Fairy?"

"Oh yes," Airy Fairy nodded, and stuck a finger in her eye. That made her eye water and her nose run.

"Then repeat what it is you have to do."

"Er..." Airy Fairy blinked and sniffed. "Clean all the rubbish and throw it out of the window."

"Great idea, Airy Fairy," giggled twin fairies Twink and Plink.

"Look out, it's raining rubbish," giggled Skelf.

All the other fairies giggled too, except Scary Fairy who just muttered, "Idiot."

Miss Stickler frowned. "Just make sure your room is spotless, Airy Fairy. Remember you only have one cleaning-up spell left."

Airy Fairy gave up trying to look intelligent and blew out her cheeks instead. She hated tidying up. She could never find anything afterwards.

"Now," went on Miss Stickler, "the other reason for calling this special meeting is to let you into a secret. It's Fairy Gropplethorpe's Rainbow Birthday in three days' time, and I want you all to magic up a present for her. Something that she'll really like. It means you'll have to work extra hard at your spelling, though. Will you do that?"

"Oh yes," said Buttercup. "I noticed Fairy Gropplethorpe needs a new red scarf. I could try to magic up that."

"And her best woolly hat blew away in the wind," said Tingle. "I could try to magic up another one."

"Huh, that's nothing," said Scary Fairy. "I am going to magic up a new cloak AND new boots for her."

"Oh..." the other fairies fell silent. It was really hard to do that.

Airy Fairy looked sadly at her wand. It was a bit wonky since she'd poked Scary Fairy with it. What could she magic up for Fairy Gropplethorpe's Rainbow Birthday? What could she magic up that Fairy Gropplethorpe would like?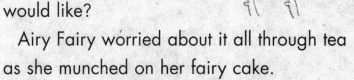

Airy Fairy worried about it all through tea as she munched on her fairy cake.

"Fairy Gropplethorpe was right," she said to Buttercup and Tingle. "There is so much to do in the springtime. First we have to spring clean our bedrooms for Miss Stickler's inspection, and I've only got one magic cleaning-up spell left. Then I have to paint my bedroom with only three magic spells. That's

really hard – I'll never win the fairy pen.
Finally I have to think up something special
for Fairy Gropplethorpe's Rainbow Birthday.
I'll never manage to do it all. I'm sure to get it
wrong."

"Stop worrying about it, Airy Fairy," said
Buttercup and Tingle. "You'll be fine."

"Oh no, you won't," muttered Scary Fairy,
listening in. "You'll be hopeless as usual. I'll
make sure of that."

Chapter Three

Later that evening, after the fairies had done their homework, they all went off to tidy their bedrooms.

"I've got to tidy mine up first time," Airy Fairy said to herself. "That's going to be tricky."

She looked around her room. It was a nice room. She had her little bed, a chair, a chest of drawers, and a big cupboard where she kept her school clothes. Sometimes. Most of the time they were over the chair, on the floor, or under the bed.

"It is a bit of a mess, I suppose," Airy Fairy muttered. "I wonder how those school socks got up on to the lightshade, and I don't remember leaving that banana skin on the floor. I'd better do as Miss Stickler says and use the tidy-up spell. Now how does it go?"

Airy Fairy thought and thought.

Is it,

Tidy up and
do it quick.

From the floor
my clothes all pick.

Or is it,
Spick and span,
span and spick.
Messy bedrooms
make me sick.

Or is it,
Everything is
in a heap.
Clean up all
I want to keep.

"Oh, I don't know," muttered Airy Fairy, and was just having a worry nibble at a fingernail when her bedroom door opened and Macduff wandered in.

Airy Fairy brightened up immediately. "Hullo, Macduff," she smiled, giving him a hug. "It's lovely to see you. You can help me tidy up, if you like."

Macduff wagged his tail and snuffled around. Airy Fairy's room was always full of good smells. He headed for Airy Fairy's bed, dived underneath, and came out crunching an old boiled sweet.

"Oh, well done, Macduff," said Airy Fairy. "I wondered where that had gone. I wonder what else is under there?" And she dived under the bed too.

"Oh look, Macduff, here's the box of chocolates Fairy Gropplethorpe gave me at Christmas time, and there are still some chocolates left. I'll share them with you so long as I can have all the coloured wrappers. I like to save them."

Macduff wagged his tail and Airy Fairy undid the foil wrappers, smoothed them out and put them into the pocket of her pink fairy frock. Then she shared out the chocolates. They were just on the last strawberry cream when they heard a voice outside in the corridor...

"Your bedroom is not too bad, Tingle, but go along to Scary Fairy's room and see what spotless really means."

"Oh no," gasped Airy Fairy, scrambling out from under the bed. "That's Miss Stickler and I haven't done any tidying at all. Now what's the right spell... I've only got one..." And she closed her eyes, waved her magic wand and said,

"Spick and span,
span and spick
Pick up everything
really quick,"
just as
Miss Stickler
came through
the door.

Immediately everything except Airy Fairy shot up into the air. Up went Macduff, the bed, the chair, the chest of drawers, the clothes that were lying about, and, worst of all, MISS STICKLER!

"Oh no," gasped Airy Fairy, as everything floated around her. "Oh no," she gasped again as her socks dropped on to Macduff's paws, and her spare knickers landed on Miss Stickler's head.

"Sorry, Miss Stickler," Airy Fairy gasped. "I'll just try another spell to make everything right..."

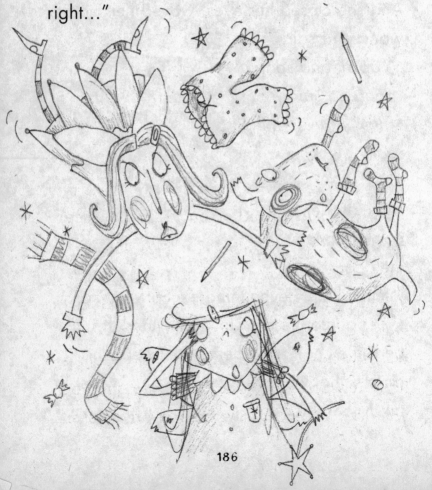

"Do NOT say another word, Airy Fairy," warned Miss Stickler, and waved her wand to put things back in place. Everything bumped down to the floor, including Miss Stickler who landed on the banana skin, skidded across the room, and hit her head on the big cupboard.

She wasn't pleased. "You are a disgrace, Airy Fairy," she stormed. "A disgrace to yourself and a disgrace to this school. When Fairy Gropplethorpe gets back, she will hear all about it. In the meantime, you will stay in every break-time till this room is tidied up and completely spotless. And you will do it WITHOUT the help of any spells.

If it's not done properly, you will not be allowed to paint your bedroom and you will lose your chance to win the special pen. Nor will you be allowed to magic up anything for Fairy Gropplethorpe's Rainbow Birthday. Do I make myself clear?"

"Yes, Miss Stickler. I'm very sorry, Miss Stickler," said Airy Fairy, and hung her head as Miss Stickler left.

To make matters worse, Scary Fairy poked her head round the door.

"What a mess," she said gleefully. "No wonder Aunt Stickler was annoyed. You'll never get to paint your bedroom now, Airy Fairy, and you'll be the only one without a present for Fairy Gropplethorpe. She won't think you're such a nice little fairy then, will she? Serves you right. I don't know why everyone likes you better than me anyway, you're such an idiot."

And Scary Fairy ran off laughing.

The other fairies heard Scary Fairy laughing and came to see what had happened.

"Oh dear," they said, when they heard.

"But don't worry, Airy Fairy," said Tingle. "I'll wash the windows for you."

"And I'll sweep the floor," said Buttercup.

"We'll all help," promised the other fairies.

Late that night, while Miss Stickler and Scary Fairy were fast asleep, the fairies flew around the silent school and gathered together buckets and mops.

Then they slipped into Airy Fairy's room and helped her spring clean. Even Macduff helped by eating up all the cake crumbs.

Airy Fairy couldn't believe it. Her bedroom had never been so tidy.

"It's not just tidy," she gasped. "It's spotless. Thank you all so much."

"That's what friends are for," smiled the other fairies, and went off to get some sleep.

But Airy Fairy couldn't sleep. She couldn't wait to show Miss Stickler her spotless bedroom. Immediately after breakfast next morning, she asked Miss Stickler to come and inspect it.

When she saw it, Miss Stickler gasped, "I don't believe it. This bedroom is almost as clean as Scary Fairy's. How did you manage it?"

"I was up all night," said Airy Fairy truthfully.

"Well, I don't know how you've done it, Airy Fairy, but your bedroom is spotless. You may now use the three spells to paint it."

"Thank you, Miss Stickler."

All the fairies were delighted for Airy Fairy, except Scary Fairy.

"How did you do it?" she scowled during morning lessons. "I bet you cheated and did some extra spells."

"No, I didn't," said Airy Fairy. "I'm hopeless at spelling. You said so yourself."

Scary Fairy scowled even harder. "You're up to something," she said. "But you'd better look out. I've got my eye on you."

But Airy Fairy didn't hear. She had closed her eyes, put her head down on her fairy notebook and was fast asleep.

Chapter Four

That afternoon Miss Stickler was in a good
mood.

"Now that all your rooms are tidy and
spotless," she said, "I've decided to give you
the afternoon off to paint them. Then we must
get on with magicking up our presents for
Fairy Gropplethorpe's Rainbow Birthday.
I hope you've been thinking about that too."

"I've been thinking there's such a lot to do,"
said Airy Fairy to Buttercup and Tingle. "I'll never
get it all done in time, and I still don't know
what to magic up for Fairy Gropplethorpe."

"Whatever it is, it'll be something stupid," said Scary Fairy. "I'm already working on my presents. The cloak and boots are going to be beautiful. Fairy Gropplethorpe's sure to like them best."

"Do stop talking, Fairies," said Miss Stickler, "and go and paint your bedrooms. Be sure to change your clothes first – and TRY not to make TOO much mess, Airy Fairy."

Airy Fairy went upstairs to her bedroom and found Macduff fast asleep on her bed.

"Poor old Macduff," she said, stroking his floppy ears. "Like me, you really do miss Fairy Gropplethorpe, don't you?"

Macduff snuffled and licked her hand.

"But you can help me decide what colour to paint my bedroom, if you like."

But Macduff just wrinkled his nose and went back to sleep.

Airy Fairy smiled. "I'll go and see what Buttercup's doing. Perhaps she'll give me an idea."

Airy Fairy tripped along the corridor to Buttercup's room and tapped on the door.

"Come in," called Buttercup.

"Ooh, Buttercup," said Airy Fairy. "Your room's lovely. It's like walking into sunshine."

"Thank you," grinned Buttercup. "I'm so glad you like it. It took all three spells to get the colour just right. What colour are you going to choose?"

"Not sure yet," said Airy Fairy. "I'm going to look at Tingle's room."

Tingle's door was wide open and Airy Fairy gasped when she saw the colour of her bedroom walls.

"Wow, Tingle!" she said. "Your room's amazing. Like a fantastic sunset."

"Thank you," said Tingle. "I'm really pleased with it, but it took all three spells to get the colour just right. What colour are you going to choose?"

"Not sure yet," sighed Airy Fairy, and wandered back along the corridor past Scary Fairy's room. Her door was open too, and her room was painted eye-watering electric pink.

Like an explosion in Mr Goblin's gobstopper factory, thought Airy Fairy.

When Scary Fairy caught sight of her, she flew out and grabbed her arm. "Have you painted your room yet?" she demanded.

"No," said Airy Fairy. "I'm not sure what colour to make it."

"Well, don't go copying mine. Pink is THE fairy colour and since I'm the best fairy, I get to choose it."

"I'll choose whatever colour I like," said Airy Fairy. "But don't worry, it won't be sickly pickly pink like yours."

"My room is NOT sickly pickly pink," said Scary Fairy and stamped her foot. "I'll turn your hair itchy twitchy witchy for that," and she raised her little wand. But Airy Fairy was too quick for her and she flipped the wand out of Scary Fairy's hand. It sailed over the bannister, twirled down to the big hall below, and rolled underneath a large table.

"How dare you!" Scary Fairy yelled. "Fetch my wand back this minute!"

"Oh, go and kiss a warty toad." Airy Fairy grinned and wandered on.

Scary Fairy made a really scary face. "I'll get you for that, Airy Fairy," she muttered. "Just see if I don't."

But Airy Fairy was too busy worrying about colours to notice.

When she got back to her room, Macduff opened one eye and yawned.

"I think I've decided on a colour," she told him. "I'm going to paint my room the colour of the sea." And she closed her eyes and said the spell,

"Turquoise blue and softest green.
Make my room a seaside dream."

ZIP! Two paint pots and two paint brushes appeared and sailed through the air towards Airy Fairy, spilling turquoise blue and softest green paint all over the floor.

"Hey, watch what you're doing!" yelled

Airy Fairy. But they didn't. They splashed
blue and green paint all over the walls and
all over the furniture.

Then, ZIP! The two paint pots and brushes
disappeared as quickly as they'd come.

"What a mess!" cried
Airy Fairy. She was
so upset, she didn't
hear Scary Fairy
giggling outside
her door.

"Oh Macduff," wailed Airy Fairy. "Just look at my room. Fairy Gropplethorpe won't be pleased and Miss Stickler will be furious. I'll have to use another spell to sort it out."

Macduff closed both eyes as Airy Fairy closed hers and said the spell,

"Clean and wipe and wipe and clean.
Make my room fit to be seen."

ZIP! Two washcloths and two buckets appeared and sailed through the air towards Airy Fairy. The wet cloths flapped about the room soaking the walls, the furniture and the floor. Soon everywhere was dripping wet.

Then, ZIP! The washcloths and the buckets left as quickly as they had come.

"Come back!" yelled Airy Fairy. "You haven't finished yet. Now my room looks worse than ever." But they didn't come back, and Airy Fairy was so upset, she didn't hear Scary Fairy giggling fit to burst outside her door.

Airy Fairy was in despair. "My room looks terrible and I only have one spell left. Oh, I wish I was better at spelling. I've got to get it right this time."

Macduff, splashed with water and paint, sat with his paws over his eyes as Airy Fairy closed her eyes and said the spell,

"Magic darkness, magic light.
Help me make my room all right."

ZIP! A large cloud appeared and enveloped Airy Fairy.

"Help help," she cried. "Where did everything go? What's happening? I can't see a thing."

Then ZIP! The cloud disappeared as quickly as it had come, and Airy Fairy looked around.

"Oh no," she cried. "I asked you to make my room all right, not all white. Now the walls are back to the colour they were to begin with."

And this time she did hear a loud laugh outside her bedroom door and just glimpsed the tip of a little wand. She opened the door wider and was just in time to see Scary Fairy disappear down the corridor. She was still laughing.

"Oh no," cried Airy Fairy. "I should have known it was Scary Fairy up to her rotten tricks. She's always getting me into trouble. Miss Stickler and Fairy Gropplethorpe will think I've been really lazy and haven't tried to paint my room at all! I can't let them think that. I must do something. But what?"

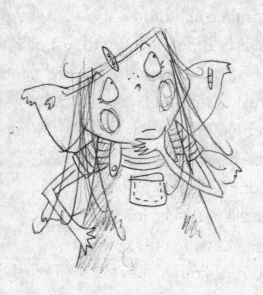

Chapter Five

For the rest of that day, Airy Fairy sat in her room and thought and thought. *How can I paint these walls in time for Fairy Gropplethorpe coming back?*

She asked the other fairies who popped in to see her. They thought and thought too.

"Sorry, Airy Fairy," they all said finally. "We've used up all our spells, so we don't know either."

Airy Fairy sighed and cuddled Macduff. He wagged his tail and knocked over her alarm clock.

Airy Fairy picked it up. "Oops, look at the time, Macduff. Time to go to the kitchen to get your supper."

Macduff wagged his tail again and followed Airy Fairy down to the kitchen. Airy Fairy went to the big store cupboard where Fairy Gropplethorpe kept his food, and looked inside. There were rows and rows of tinned dog food. Macduff shuffled forward and snuffled at a tin on the bottom row.

"Do you want that one?" asked Airy Fairy. Macduff wagged his tail and Airy Fairy pulled out the tin. All the other tins of dog food collapsed in a heap round about her.

"Oh no," she wailed. "Everything is in a mess today."

But then she saw some other tins piled up behind the dog food.

"Paint tins," breathed Airy Fairy. "With different colours of paint. I could choose one of those, and paint my room myself. Fairy Gropplethorpe wouldn't mind." And she lifted out a sky blue one and looked inside. "I like the colour," she said,"but there's not enough paint left to paint my room. I'll try the soft lilac one. I like that colour too." And she lifted it down and looked inside. "Oh no, there's not enough paint left in that one either."

She tried all the other paint tins, but they were all the same. None of them had enough paint left to paint a fairy bedroom.

While Macduff munched his supper Airy Fairy sat down among the paint tins to have a think. She looked at the names on the tins. Sky Blue. Soft Lilac. Sunshine Yellow. Spring Green. SPRING GREEN! Airy Fairy jumped up.

"That's it, Macduff," she cried. "I've got it. I'll use all the colours in the paint pots to paint my bedroom."

Later that night, when everyone else was fast asleep, Macduff watched as Airy Fairy flew up and down the stairs carrying as many paint pots as she could.

"That should do it," she puffed, as she looked at all the tins in the middle of her bedroom floor. "Now what should I begin with?" Then she remembered how nice the school had looked in the spring sunshine. She remembered the bowls of spring flowers in the hall, and she remembered the fat buds on the oak tree. And she smiled, dipped her paintbrush into the first pot and began to paint.

Dawn was lightening the sky by the time
she had finished and ferried all the paint pots
back to the store, and it was a very sleepy
Airy Fairy who sat down at her desk for
morning lessons.

Scary Fairy poked her awake with her
wand. "Have you decided on a colour to
paint your bedroom yet?" she giggled.

"Why are you asking?" said Airy Fairy. "You
know very well you magicked up a mess."

"But you can't prove it," smirked Scary Fairy. "And I bet Fairy Gropplethorpe will be really cross with you for not even TRYING to win the special pen." And she sat back, looking very pleased with herself.

Two minutes later Miss Stickler came bustling into the classroom. "Fairies, Fairies," she cried. "A terrible thing has happened. It seems I have made a mistake."

The fairies all looked at each other. Miss Stickler make a mistake? That had never happened before.

"I have got the date of Fairy Gropplethorpe's Rainbow Birthday wrong. I thought it was tomorrow, but it's not, it's today. Fairy Gropplethorpe will be back from her conference shortly, and I must organize her birthday tea. This morning, therefore, you must finish off your special presents for her. I hope you're all making something really nice." And she hurried off to the kitchen to make a birthday cake.

"I'm glad my scarf for Fairy Gropplethorpe's nearly finished," said Buttercup. "I just have to work out the spell for putting some fringes on the ends."

"My woolly hat's nearly finished too," said Tingle. "I just have to work out the spell for putting a bobble on the top."

"My cloak and boots have been finished for ages," boasted Scary Fairy. "But then I am the best at spelling, as well as everything else."

And she turned to Airy Fairy and said.
"What have you made for Fairy
Gropplethorpe's Rainbow Birthday? I bet it's
something stupid."

"No, it's not," said Airy Fairy, "because
I've had so much to do, I haven't made
anything yet."

"Then you'll be the only one without
anything for Fairy Gropplethorpe. You really
are in trouble, Airy Fairy. Serves you right.
You're such an idiot!" And Scary Fairy flew
away laughing.

Chapter Six

Airy Fairy sat and listened to what all the other fairies were making for Fairy Gropplethorpe's Rainbow Birthday. Cherri was making her a new shopping basket. Twin fairies Twink and Plink were making her new gloves, one each. Honeysuckle had designed a fantastic frilly parasol. "For the sunny days ahead," she smiled. And Silvie and Skelf were working on a matching necklace and bracelet.

"What does that leave for me to make?" wondered Airy Fairy. And she sat in the classroom, with her elbows on her desk and her chin in her hands, after the others had gone.

She looked out of the window. The oak buds had just burst and tiny green leaves were stretching themselves out towards the sunshine.

"I knew they would do that when I wasn't looking," she said.

And she was so busy looking at the new leaves, she didn't notice Scary Fairy keeping an eye on her through the classroom door.

But she did notice the red squirrel leaping around among the branches of the oak tree.

"Hullo, Mr Squirrel," she called. "I'd love to come out and play with you, but I've got to magic up a present for Fairy Gropplethorpe's Rainbow Birthday, and I don't know what to make." Then she noticed the red squirrel nibbling away on a nut and that gave her an idea.

"I know what I can do," she cried. "I can magic up some chocolates for Fairy Gropplethorpe. She likes chocolates." And Airy Fairy closed her eyes and said the spell,

"Creamy-centred luscious chocs.
Send them down
in a pretty box."

THUNK! A large
brown box dropped
on to the floor.

"Oh dear," said
Airy Fairy. "That
doesn't look like
what I asked for."

THIS WAY UP

She peeped inside. It wasn't a box of chocs. It was a box of rocks. Big ones, small ones, jaggy ones, craggy ones.

"Now how did that happen?" said Airy Fairy. "I was sure I had got the spell right. Perhaps I had better look up Miss Stickler's Big Book of Spells to check."

Outside the classroom door, Scary Fairy giggled. "That won't do you any good. Not while I'm around."

Airy Fairy was just looking through the Big Book of Spells when she had another idea.

"Fairy Gropplethorpe loves books. I could magic up a Big Book of Fairy Tales for her Rainbow Birthday."

And she closed her eyes and said the spell,

"Stories of giants, mermaids and whales.
I'd like a Big Book of Fairy Tales."

WHUMP! A whole pile of hairy tails fell down. There were curly ones, straight ones, stripy ones and spiky ones.

"Oi, get off me!" yelled Airy Fairy. "I'm sure I didn't ask for hairy tails."

Outside the classroom door, Scary Fairy was laughing fit to burst. She was having a great time upsetting Airy Fairy's spells.

But Airy Fairy wasn't giving up.

"Well, magicking up a box of chocs and a book haven't got me anywhere," she muttered. "What else would Fairy Gropplethorpe like?"

She thought and thought. *She's already getting a cloak and boots, a hat and scarf, a parasol and gloves, a necklace and bracelet, and a basket. What else is there?*

"I know," she cried. "Perfume. Fairy Gropplethorpe likes to dab a little behind her ears. I'll do the spell for that."

And she closed her eyes and said the spell,
"Roses, pansies, scented flocks.
Send some perfume in a box."
EUGH! It started raining smelly socks.

"Oh no," wailed Airy Fairy. "I'm sure I didn't ask for smelly socks."

Outside the classroom door, Scary Fairy was holding her sides. Then she saw Miss Stickler coming round the corner and she flew away, sharpish. Miss Stickler hurried along to the classroom.

"Help," she cried, as she tripped over the box of rocks and landed in among the pile of hairy tails and smelly socks.

"Airy Fairy!" she yelled. "I might have guessed. If there's a mess, you're bound to be responsible for it."

"But I was only trying to magic up a present for Fairy Gropplethorpe's Rainbow Birthday," protested Airy Fairy.

"Too late for that now," said Miss Stickler. "Fairy Gropplethorpe has arrived. Now hurry along to the hall and take your place with the other fairies for the Rainbow Birthday surprise."

Airy Fairy went along to the hall. All the other fairies were there with their presents. The presents looked beautiful, especially Scary Fairy's cloak and boots.

"See what I magicked up for Fairy Gropplethorpe," she said. "A bit better than a box of rocks or hairy tails or smelly socks, isn't it, Airy Fairy?"

Airy Fairy sighed. She should have watched out for Scary Fairy.

Then Fairy Gropplethorpe came into the hall, followed by Macduff, nearly wagging his tail off. He was so pleased to see her.

"Happy Rainbow Birthday!" all the fairies cried, and to Fairy Gropplethorpe's surprise and delight, they presented her with their gifts.

Airy Fairy hung back. She had nothing to give Fairy Gropplethorpe for her special birthday. Then she looked at Macduff and remembered sitting on the floor of her bedroom with him, eating the last of the Christmas chocolates. Then she remembered putting the coloured foil wrappers in her pocket.

Then she had an idea. She took the
wrappers out and secretly made them into
a neat little shape. That done, she smiled,
closed her eyes and whispered the spell,

"Not a glove, not a hat,
not a bright woolly mitten.
Please send me down
a small rainbow kitten."

MIAOW. At her feet appeared the tiniest,
stripiest kitten Airy Fairy had ever seen.
Airy Fairy grinned, picked
her up, and took her to
Fairy Gropplethorpe.

"Happy Rainbow Birthday, Fairy Gropplethorpe!" she said. "I hope you like the rainbow kitten. I hope Macduff likes her too. He was a little bit lonely while you were away."

"Oh, thank you, Airy Fairy," beamed Fairy Gropplethorpe. "How thoughtful of you. I just love her. I'll call her Rainbow, of course. What do you think, Macduff?"

Macduff gave a big happy WUFF! and wagged his tail in circles.

Scary Fairy scowled. How had Airy Fairy managed it? It was easy to see Fairy Gropplethorpe really liked the kitten.

"Let's have the birthday tea now," said Miss Stickler. "I've made you a special cake, Fairy Gropplethorpe."

"Oh, can't we show Fairy Gropplethorpe our newly painted bedrooms first, Aunt Stickler?" said Scary Fairy. She was sure THAT would get Airy Fairy into trouble and she was sure SHE would win the special pen.

"Of course," said Miss Stickler. "I'd nearly forgotten." And she led the way upstairs.

Fairy Gropplethorpe was delighted at how neat and clean and bright the newly painted bedrooms were.

"You've had so much to do and you've worked very hard," she said to the fairies. "Well done."

"Just wait till she gets to your room," Scary Fairy smirked to Airy Fairy.

Airy Fairy's bedroom was last, and when Miss Stickler opened the door, everyone gasped. Inside it was springtime. On one white wall, Airy Fairy had painted a large oak tree, and

nestling in its branches was Fairy
Gropplethorpe's Academy for Good Fairies.
Spring sunshine shone on the school, making
its windows sparkle. On the branches, green
leaves were just opening up, and ten tiny
fairies and a red squirrel played among
them. On a sturdy branch sat Miss Stickler,
Fairy Gropplethorpe and Macduff, while
underneath, a spring garden bloomed. The
garden wound its way round the other walls
where Airy Fairy had painted little animals
and birds playing
in the spring
sunshine.

Fairy Gropplethorpe clapped her hands.
"Oh, how splendid, Airy Fairy," she said.
"What a wonderful idea."

"I had to use the spare paint from the tins
in the cupboard downstairs because my
spells didn't work out very well," said Airy
Fairy truthfully.

"Then you've worked really hard indeed,"
smiled Fairy Gropplethorpe. "I don't think
there's any doubt that this is the best
bedroom, and that Airy Fairy deserves the
prize. Don't you agree, Miss Stickler?"

Miss Stickler opened her mouth to protest, then just nodded. Scary Fairy made a face that was really scary.

"But I'm afraid, before you get the special pen, Airy Fairy, you'll have to get the paint tins out again because there's something you've forgotten to put in the picture."

Airy Fairy looked all round the walls. She screwed up her eyes and looked all round again.

"I don't know…"

Buttercup and Tingle smiled at each other and nudged Airy Fairy. "Miaow," they giggled.

"Oh, I know what it is now." Airy Fairy grinned. "I've still to paint in a rainbow kitten."

Meet Airy Fairy.

Her wand is all wonky, her wings
are covered in sticking plaster
and her spells are always a muddle!
But she's the cutest fairy around!

Look out for the other
books in this series.

Margaret Ryan

Airy Fairy

Magic Mix-Up!

How can one little
fairy get into such
BIG trouble?

SCHOLASTIC

Margaret Ryan

Airy Fairy

Magic Mistakes!

How can one little
fairy get into such
BIG trouble?

SCHOLASTIC

Margaret Ryan

Airy Fairy

Magic Music!

How can one little
fairy get into such
BIG trouble?

SCHOLASTIC